The Blue Cat
of Castle Town

Catherine Cate Coblentz
Illustrated by Janice Holland

Dover Publications, Inc.
Mineola, New York

Bibliographical Note

This Dover edition, first published in 2017, is an unabridged republication
of the work originally published by the Countryman Press, Woodstock,
Vermont, in 1949.

International Standard Book Number

ISBN-13: 978-0-486-81527-5
ISBN-10: 0-486-81527-7

Manufactured in the United States by LSC Communications
81527701   2017
www.doverpublications.com

CONTENTS

To
MARY GERRISH HIGLEY
*the teacher who carefully sought out
and preserved the source material of
Castleto'n, Vermont,
and to*
HULDA COLE
*the librarian who loaned the
material to the author and who helped
find the answers to many questions*

CHAPTER ONE

The Blue Cat
of Castle Town

No one knows why the word Castle was chosen as the name for the Town.

— From a Historian's note.

THE BLUE CAT OF CASTLE TOWN

Once in a blue moon there comes
A cat that is blue,
Singing the river's song,
Seeking — for you!

THE blue kitten was born under a blue moon in a warm nest of dried clover, Queen Anne's lace and chickory, which his mother had made for him at the foot of a forgotten haycock in a Vermont meadow. It was the end of the first third of the nineteenth century, or more than a hundred years ago, which is a very long time indeed.

The mother cat had been quite upset when she first saw the blue kitten. She had looked fearfully then toward the river. For, like all cats, she had heard that a blue kitten could learn the river's song.

Any kitten has a hard enough time to find a home for himself. For every kitten must find a hearth to fit his song. But a kitten who listens to the river and learns the river's song has the hardest time of all.

Not only must the kitten who sings the river's song find a hearth to fit that song, but he must teach the keeper of that hearth to sing the same song. The river's song is very old. And mortals who have ears to hear and hearts to sing are fewer than few.

Yet such folk must be found at least once in a blue moon. For if the river's song rise no longer from the hearthside, then it is said, the very days of the land itself are numbered.

So a blue kitten is like a knight, a small knight sent forth on a quest, armed only with a song. There are great rewards for knights and kittens who succeed. But no one has ever told what happens to those who fail.

Small wonder the mother cat was afraid. Still, when she found three black hairs on the end of the kitten's tail she was a bit more hopeful. For as long as a blue kitten has even one black hair, there is a chance that he will live and die an ordinary cat. "And after all," the mother cat consoled herself, "my kitten has three black hairs, *three!*" She counted them again to be sure she was right.

"Do not listen to the river," she warned the blue kitten, as soon as his eyes were wide open and he was old enough to pay attention. "Remember, grasshoppers make you thin. Moles are indigestible. While birds should be killed only when no mortal is looking. Yet though these are important matters, still it is permitted that now and then you may forget. But — whatever you do, never listen to the river!"

She turned her back on him then and stalked off, as though she could not bear to tell him any more. Only her tail stood up, straight and tall, moving through the grass stubble, like a horrible warning.

The blue kitten watched, head on one side, his amber

eyes puzzled. Perhaps if his mother had turned back and told him why he must not listen, things might have turned out differently. One never knows.

For a long time, however, the kitten paid no attention to the river's far-off murmuring. Perhaps he thought it all part of the sound of summer, surging up, sweeping down, or wafted over the nest of dried clover, Queen Anne's lace and chickory.

Besides, the kitten was busy with the business of growing up, which meant playing with a timothy tassel, watching a spider looping his web, or wondering whether for one wonderful second he had really seen the pointed nose and the bright eyes of a field mouse.

The river bided its time. Every day, however, its murmur grew a trifle louder. Oh, the least bit louder. Until one morning the kitten pricked up his blue ears, which deep inside were pink like sea shells. Was that low sound someone talking? Then, as the pointed tips of his ears bent forward, simple, lovely words slipped in, past the blue tips, down into the sea-shell pinkness, like so many notes of music, spilled from the bobolink.

"Castle Town, where I am going, is a lovely town," came the words. "Nobody knows why it is called Castle Town. But everybody, even a blue kitten, knows that castles are enchanted."

The blue kitten nodded his head. "Yes, wind," he said. "Castles are enchanted." Naturally, living in a meadow, he understood a good deal about enchantment.

"There have even been some folk in Castle Town," the murmur continued, "and there is one there now, who would break this enchantment. Enchantment is made up of three things — of beauty, peace and content."

"Beauty, peace and content," purred the blue kitten, thinking of the wonder of the meadow.

"The one who would break the enchantment," went on the soft, slow sound, "does not see beauty. He has no peace. He is not content."

The blue kitten shook his head sadly. Two tears dropped from his amber eyes.

"Not content," he said.

"More than that, he is weaving a dark spell." The murmur was so low and so sad that the kitten put his head close to the grass roots to listen.

"Out of greed for gold and power is the dark spell being woven. And if the folk in Castle Town yield to this spell, and do not listen to our song, then the glory of Castle Town will be lost forever."

It was difficult for the blue kitten to hear. Perhaps if his ears were larger. Or perhaps if he sat up straight. He tried that. Sure enough he could hear much better. Over the widespread leaves of the meadow sorrel, in a low, sweet whisper came the words, "If the glory of Castle Town be not lost forever, you must find some there, blue kitten, who will listen to our song."

"Listen to our song." The blue kitten nodded, watching the sorrel nodding too. "Listen . . ." He stopped and asked sharply, "Are you the wind?"

"I am the river," came the murmur. "And you will listen to me!"

"Will listen to you," replied the kitten.

Suddenly he remembered his mother. "She said . . ." wailed the kitten.

"It is too late now," replied the river. "Besides, you will discover that you hear me whether you listen or no. So, listen well, and some time I will teach you The Song. But first, I shall tell you of Castle Town."

"I — will — not — listen!" declared the blue kitten

stoutly, putting two blue paws firmly over both ears. Kitten paws do make good ear muffs, but they are warm. And summer is no time for a kitten to wear ear muffs, at least not for long.

When he removed the paws, just to cool his ears, the river was laughing at him. "You are not a blue kitten for nothing," it said, and went right on murmuring. But now it was only a comforting, soothing hum, just part of the meadow's enchantment and wonder.

After that the blue kitten really tried not to listen. But of course no kitten can keep his ears covered all the time. And little by little, day after day, he heard the sound of the river. Every now and then it told of Castle Town.

"Castle Town was settled a long time ago," said the river. "Up from Connecticut, through the wilderness, came men and women, riding on horseback or walking beside their oxcarts.

"They brought their Bibles and their babies in their arms. They brought apple seeds and rose roots, which had come long ago from England and from Scotland, in their

saddlebags. They brought seed corn and barley. They brought axes and tools and pewter molds, spinning wheels and looms in their carts."

"And they brought my seven-times great grandfather in a little girl's pocket," interrupted the kitten. His mother, when she had been in a story-telling mood — which was not often — had told him that.

The river paid no attention. Perhaps the river knew more about the kitten's seven-times great grandfather than the kitten — or even his mother, knew.

"Best of all," declared the river, "these folk from Connecticut brought the Bright Enchantment. Beauty and peace and content they brought in their hearts. They knew, and some among them sang, the river's song.

"So they came to the Vermont valley and said that here should be their castle forever. For a man's home is his castle. They cleared the land, they planted their corn and barley. They slipped the apple seeds hopefully in the earth, and they set out their rose roots near the log cabins which were their first homes.

"Soon the cabins gave place to homes of boards of pine, of maple and of birch. Some of these homes were set close together for company, along a mile of road which ran east and west through the valley. At the east end of this mile was the village green so the children of Castle Town should have a place to play forever. The church was built on the edge of the green and a graveyard was beside it for the dead to rest in. Not far from the center of this settled mile was a tavern, where men often gathered and talked much of liberty. And at the west end was the cobbler's shop. The bricks in the walls of that shop were the softest rose color, folk said, in all the world — or at least in as much of the world as they had seen. The boards which went into the homes in the valley were the finest, the apples which soon hung on the apple boughs were a much better flavor than they had even been in Connecticut. And as for juice — well you had only to taste the cider to judge that! While the fragrance lifting from the roses was such a sweet, though unseen, cloud that it made the hearts of all those passing through it beat faster, and their feet kept time as to music.

"All this was part of the Bright Enchantment in the days when there was beauty and peace and content in the hearts of the people of Castle Town."

In spite of himself the blue kitten began to purr, "Beauty and peace and content."

"What did I tell you?" cried the mother cat, coming to the haycock at that very moment with a field mouse. And she smacked the blue kitten sharply on his right ear. And even more sharply on the left, for that was the ear nearest the river.

But it was too late. The blue kitten was growing fast. And, the river had been right, for whether he listened or not, he heard it murmuring. Day after day he heard it. Most of all he heard the words, "Beauty and peace and content." He would like to find a hearth where a mortal understood and sang that song.

"It will not be easy," warned the river. "Occasionally there have been men and women who were born knowing the song, but mortals cannot teach it to other mortals. Only a blue cat can do that, a blue cat who sings and believes in the song."

"Believes — what is that?" asked the kitten.

"That is something you must find out for yourself. Not even I, the river, can tell you. But this I can say. Castle Town needs to learn the song and that quickly if the dark spell, which is now being fashioned, is to be kept from engulfing the place. So your quest, blue kitten, is very important. Remember, you must live your own life, and sing your own song.

"Now, whatever happens, and plenty will happen, do not be discouraged too easily or too soon. Your task is hard and there will be many difficulties to face. But this, too, is true, blue kitten, if you do find a mortal who will welcome you at the hearthstone, and who will both listen and sing the song as long as you live, not only shall you rest in comfort in your chosen place, but you shall live forever!"

"Live forever," echoed the blue kitten.

"That is utter nonsense," declared his mother, when the kitten told her he was going to live forever. "Never have I heard of a cat with more than nine lives! Never!"

"But the river . . ." began the kitten.

"Mer-row! I see you would rather listen to the river than to me," said the blue kitten's mother sadly. And she sat and looked at nothing for a long time.

At last she came to a decision. "Very well, blue kitten!" she said. "The moon will be blue tomorrow night. So, as long as you are determined upon it, you had better go then and sit in the reeds by the river's edge and learn the river's song. It must be done, if it is to be done at all, in a single night.

"Besides," she continued, "you will be grown soon and there are no longer enough mice in the meadow to feed the two of us. So perhaps it is just as well that you get ready now to make your way in the world."

"But," began the blue kitten, thinking how full of mouse his stomach was, and how soothing it was to have his whiskers brushed, "the river says my task is hard and there will be many difficulties."

"Of course," agreed the mother. "I told you that a long time ago. Or at any rate I told you not to listen to the river. But, after all, a nest of dried clover, Queen Anne's lace and chickory cannot last forever. You must live your own life and sing your own song."

"That's just what the river says," declared the kitten.

"Mer-row! Oh, go and listen to the river then!" said the mother cat crossly.

CHAPTER TWO
The River's Song

Sing your own song. Sing well.
— From the River's Song.

THE RIVER'S SONG

THE blue kitten curled his blue tail respectfully around him and sat facing the river. It had been dusk when he left the comfort of the familiar haycock and set forth. But it was almost dark when he came through the reeds and by the wild duck's nest to the edge of the river. He heard the heavy flapping of wings as the startled duck whirred upward. He heard the hoot owl on a dead limb, and the lonely call of the whippoorwill. He wiggled the toes of his front paws wistfully. He did so want to turn about and go home.

But he didn't. He only made his homesick toes be still, sat a little straighter, curled his tail a little closer, and waited.

Both his ears were bent forward to listen. But the river was paying no attention whatever to the blue kitten. It gurgled and hissed and splattered along over the stones — splattered and hissed and gurgled. Not until the blue moon began to peer over the mountain did the river hush gradually into quiet. Only when — like a great cat's-eye — the moon was clear of the mountain and its light reflected all along the water, the river began to sing — a song the kitten had never heard.

And the kitten, a little dark shadow in the moonlight, felt the song slipping into his ears, along his backbone, and tingling even the tips of his four paws and the end of his tail.

Yet this was strange. For the song itself was as simple and wonderful as life in a meadow. Beauty and peace and content were there. And a glory flooding over — like the light of the blue moon shining around the blue kitten.

"*Sing your own song*, said the river.
Sing your own song.

"*Out of yesterday song comes.*
It goes into tomorrow,
Sing your own song.

"*With your life fashion beauty,*
This too is the song.
Riches will pass and power. Beauty remains.
Sing your own song.

"*All that is worth doing, do well*, said the river.
Sing your own song.
Certain and round be the measure,
Every line be graceful and true.
Time is the mold, time the weaver, the carver,
Time and the workman together,
Sing your own song.
"*Sing well*, said the river. *Sing well.*"

"Purr," went the kitten, slowly and carefully. "Purr, purr, purrr." That was the first line.

But as he finished it, the blue kitten suddenly felt afraid. So he began to bargain with the river. Being a blue kitten, he was wiser than most.

"Before you teach me the rest of the song, river," he begged, "help me a little. There must be many people in Castle Town. Tell me about them so I shall know whom to choose."

The river gurgled before answering. No one had ever questioned the river in this manner, and therefore it was a little uncertain as to how much even a blue kitten should know. Finally, however, the river began, slowly and soothingly.

"Well, there is a pewterer in Castle Town. His name is Southmayd. Ebenezer is the first name. Once he sang the song. But of late he has forgotten. Still he has ears which should recognize the song when he hears it again. And it is possible there is yet a tune in his throat. And magic in his hands. Though whether he has time enough to fashion beauty, being only a river, I cannot say."

"Um!" said the kitten, nodding his head. "Southmayd, Ebenezer."

"There is a weaver in Castle Town," went on the river, "who came from Ireland. He has never sung the song, but once he dreamed of singing it. If you could only get him started, who knows? The hearth you are seeking might be there. The name of the weaver is John Gilroy."

"Gil — roy," said the kitten sleepily. "John. Ho — ho — hum!" He opened his mouth so wide and tipped his head so far back one would have thought he expected to swallow the stars.

"Ho — ho — hum!" After all the kitten had never before been long away from the warm nest of dried clover, Queen Anne's lace and chickory. Nor tried to stay awake all night for that matter. While naturally the light of a blue moon is soothing.

He meant to listen very carefully. But the voice of the river was gentle and slow. The cat settled down and closed his eyes so the light of the blue moon on the waters should not distract him. And almost at once he began to sink deeper and deeper into the dark velvet softness of a kitten's sleep.

But the river was too busy telling its secrets to notice. Or perhaps it did notice and thought — Well, after all, I am keeping my part of the bargain.

"Beware of Arunah Hyde," it whispered. "Beware! Never sing your song to him. Take heed of what I say, blue kitten. For you and Arunah work different spells. Arunah loves gold very much. And the dark spell he is fashioning has him in its clutches. He seeks after something and knows not what, so he seeks the more desperately. His hands are full and spilling over with gold. But his heart is empty of beauty and peace. He has never known content.

"The top whirls fast and yet faster,
  Till it falls, slung wide from its whirling.
  The spring wound too tight will break from the straining.

"There is Bright Enchantment and man is its master.
  And there is dark seeking forever, and that masters the
    man."

So sang the river. "Forever and ever, and ever."

By this time the kitten's nose was buried deep in his paws, and he sighed a little in his sleep. While the wind swept through the valley in a long, dreary moan.

The river spoke a little louder. "And in trying to rid himself of the dark spell, Arunah is but spreading it. Arunah is planning now to make Castle Town the center of the Vermont Universe."

The blue kitten opened his eyes and shook the river spray from his whiskers.

"Vermont? Universe?" he asked sharply.

"It is all the same," declared the river. "Any Vermonter will tell you so."

"Ah," said the kitten. And he curled down once more and drew the dark, soft sleep back over him like a shawl. But this time the tip of his left ear stuck out, and it did hear a little. Though the kitten was not to remember for a long, long while what the left ear heard.

The river took up its murmuring. "So, whatever you do, blue kitten, beware of Arunah Hyde. Never, I warn you, sing your song to him. Arunah, too, has a song. And that spreads his dark enchantment. One of you will win in the end, for on your two songs does the future of Castle Town depend. And in the end, too, one of you will be over-powered by his own song."

Had the kitten been awake — really awake, he would have cried out like his mother that such words were non-sense.

"Now, remember, the name is Arunah Hyde," repeated the river. Then, with a sharp swish, it flung a dash of cold water over the small form curled by the reeds. "Did you hear what I said, blue kitten?"

"Of course," sniffed the kitten with a shiver, sitting up now very straight. "His name is Arunah Hyde."

"Mm!" came from the river. "Beware too of the man who wants office because he thinks the office will make him important."

"Of course," yawned the kitten.

"And of the loud talker, the one who wants to show off and have things better than his neighbors."

The kitten yawned again. This time as his head tipped back he saw the blue moon. It was climbing fast. It was right above him.

"Have you told me all I should know?" he asked the river.

"All, blue kitten? Why, I am just beginning."

The kitten did not like the tone. He lifted his head and stared across the river as though much interested in the bushes on the other side. "After all," he said loftily, "I am the blue kitten. And I can learn some things for myself!"

But the river went on as though it had not been interrupted.

"There is a carpenter in Castle Town, a simple man, and no one knows him well. Yet he, like yourself, was born to the sound of the river's singing. His father was a silversmith. And he sang the song well. But when he wanted to teach his son to work with silver, the son would not listen. Yet the sound of the river's song is forever in the son's ears. Perhaps you will meet this man."

"The name?" demanded the blue kitten, who was getting very weary. Besides the blue moon was moving toward the west. And when the moon should disappear, he understood — for his mother had warned him — he must have learned the river's song. Blue moons come seldom in a kitten's life. Or in anyone else's for that matter.

"The name is Thomas Royal Dake. His mother gave him the name Thomas. But his father insisted on Royal. That," explained the river, "is a term applied to kings."

"But this man is only a carpenter."

"Only a carpenter," agreed the river. It lingered over the syllables, as though it loved them.

"Dake," said the blue kitten. "Thomas."

"Royal," added the river.

"Umph," sniffed the kitten. "Is there anyone else in Castle Town whom I should know?"

"Well, there is a girl in Castle Town, who is not anything at all. She is not rich and she is not pretty. And she has an ugly name. She is lonely, for her mother is dead. I know nothing about her voice, but she has an ear for sounds. She listens to the wind, and to the gurgle of the brook, or so I am told. So, she might listen to you. She . . ."

"We had better get on with the song," said the blue kitten, not bothering to learn the girl's name. For the moon had passed its zenith.

"Oh, well," groaned the river, "there are some things, small kitten, which as you say, you must learn for yourself. Most certainly you will have a hard time. But it is not my fault — not really!"

Now, the blue kitten of Castle Town was smarter than

most. Of course being blue had something to do with it. So by the time the blue moon took its last look across the valley before slipping out of sight, the blue kitten had learned all the river's song, that song as old as the world itself. For the Creator of All Things was the first to sing it.

Only as he was leaving, the river said a trifle contemptuously, "After all, you may turn out to be only an ordinary cat."

"An ordinary cat!" Sniff, went the blue kitten who had learned the river's song. "An ordinary cat!" The very idea!

In the dawn his mother was waiting for him by the haycock. She washed his face for the last time, taking good care that his ears were clean. Pink ears are so becoming to a blue cat. She looked thoughtfully at his fine, long, white whiskers and at the eyebrows which sprouted up like two small fountains above his amber eyes. She approved of the softness and whiteness of his waistcoat. That was the result of a good diet. The very last thing she did was to count the black hairs on the end of his tail.

"After all," she said then thoughtfully, "you may turn out to be an ordinary cat."

Then the blue kitten, who didn't for an instant believe these words, walked proudly out of the meadow. Even before the sun rose he was on his way to Castle Town to find a mortal who would listen to his singing and would learn the river's song. And he was, the blue kitten assured himself, he was the *blue kitten*. And some day he would be the *blue cat*. That was not an ordinary thing. Not by any manner of means! Pssst! The idea!

Ebenezer Southmayd, THE PEWTERER

You will find as the touchmark of this pewterer
the initials E.S. below a full-rigged ship.
— From a book about pewter
and pewter makers in America.

EBENEZER SOUTHMAYD, THE PEWTERER

JUST outside Castle Town the blue kitten saw a narrow lane leading off from the main road and meandering over a hill. At the bend of the lane a wisp of smoke was rising from a chimney. The house itself, he decided, was hidden by the thicket of cherry and alder. Sitting in the dust of the main road and gazing at the smoke, the kitten found all the teaching of the river and his mother coming to his aid so that he could understand even the ways of mortals. Smoke meant a fire. And fire, with mortals, meant food. And a hearth for a most important blue kitten.

Having come to this conclusion, he stood up and hastened along the lane. A young tabby, in the doorway of the barn next to the small, unpainted house, stopped washing her face to watch him. But, beyond noticing that she was an ordinary yellow cat, the blue kitten paid no attention. After all, a barn cat was scarcely in his category. Instead, holding his head and tail high, he marched straight to the doorstone at one end of the house and sat down expectantly. When nothing happened he began to demand admittance, his tone growing louder and louder.

A girl opened the door and looked at him. She is very ugly, thought the kitten. But then I suppose mortals can't be as beautiful as cats. After all she may have a good hearthstone.

He peered around her and into the room. It was the first room the kitten had seen. But by virtue of his color and his association with the river, as well as his long days in the meadow, he could list everything at once.

A table, with no cover. Two straight chairs, never made for a cat to curl in. A spinning wheel in one corner and a cobweb or two. A hearth, yes. But nothing comfortable there on which a blue kitten could properly lie. Not even a decent fire, for the wood burned sullenly as though minded to go out any minute. The kettle on the crane above gave forth no comfortable humming. A mortal's house, decided the kitten, certainly lacked the comforts of a meadow.

Yet, disappointed though he was, the blue kitten sat down on the doorstone and started the river's song.

"Go away," said the girl sharply at the very first purr. "Go away."

But the blue kitten finished one line.

Then the door slammed in his face. He thought he heard a sob, but he was too provoked to care. The idea of not letting him in! Of not at least giving him a good breakfast! Was he not the blue kitten? And could he not sing the river's song?

A sheep in the pasture beyond spoke disdainfully, but the young tabby in the barn doorway mewed in a friendly fashion. The kitten paid no attention. Instead, after huffing himself up and up to show how provoked he was, he turned about. And looking neither to the right nor to the

left, he marched down the lane and back to the road, which he had so hopefully left such a short time before. Then on and on he padded, on and on, until he came to the edge of the town, and the edge of the village green as well.

"Now I am in the part of Castle Town where the houses are set close together for company," he said to himself. "Let me see. I should look, the river told me, for Ebenezer Southmayd, John Gilroy, Arunah Hyde or — oh, well, a carpenter and a girl. But surely one of these first mortals will listen and sing the song. I shall not need to remember the whole list."

After all, decided the blue kitten, stopping to admire himself in a well at the edge of the village green, after all,

I am a good-looking kitten. Anyone — anyone at all, except of course that ugly girl in her ugly house — will be glad to listen to me!

He leaned over farther to see whether his whiskers and his eyebrows were in order. A little farther, and suddenly the waters of the well fairly rushed up to meet him. There was a loud splash.

And there he was, in the cold and wet, going down and down.

He managed to give one wild despairing yowl before the waters closed over him completely. He had no time to shut his eyes, and he glimpsed for one brief moment a man's face framed in white hair, peering at him from the rim of the well.

Then with a terrible creaking and groaning something began to move down and down, closer and closer. The blue kitten was too frightened now even to use his knowledge and good judgment. Instead he sensed only a mighty fear which his ancestors had sometimes known. There was no doubt about it, this must be the dark spell coming to swallow him up. That would be a fate far worse than drowning.

The creaking and groaning stopped, and sure enough the spell was beneath him, was all around him, was fairly scooping him in. I am about to be digested, like a mouse, decided the kitten. And I shall never, never know a hearth to fit my song. Oh, dear! Why did I ever, ever listen to the river?

The creaking and the groaning, which was really the sound of a windlass, began again. Now the blue kitten was being lifted up and up. Then the loaded bucket filled with its strange burden was seized and turned over. And the kitten was dumped on the grass. There he lay, on the village green, looking more like a sopping wet dishcloth than a blue kitten.

So that was the way the blue kitten was introduced into Castle Town. Dipped, like a piece of trash, out of a well! It was most humiliating.

The kitten felt terribly ashamed of himself. But the man with the white hair framing his face, picked him up — as cats should be picked up — by the scruff of his neck. With water dripping from his chin, his tail, his paws, and even from the tips of his ears, he was carried through a door and put down, gently enough, on a hearth beside a brick furnace. The bricks felt warm and almost at once a comfortable feeling began to creep along the cat's backbone.

Still he lay there, sprawled out, pretending he was half-drowned, which he wasn't at all. He hadn't been in the water long enough to be even a quarter-drowned, or an eighth-drowned, for that matter. But, being sorry for himself, he wanted the man with the white hair to be sorry too.

He had, the kitten recalled, been told that his task would be hard and there would be many difficulties. But he had never dreamed it would be as difficult as this.

Finally the kitten opened one eye and then the other. There were little shadows dancing on the floor. And looking above him for an instant he saw that the bricks against which he leaned held an open furnace — something, he

supposed, like a blacksmith's forge in the shop where his mother had boasted of once overpowering a fine young rat. Over the furnace was a sheltering hood. The whole effect was unquestionably, in the kitten's mind, very cozy indeed.

Then his whiskers twitched, remindingly, and he brought his head down. Right in front of him stood a porringer full of milk. The kitten lapped up the last drop, and with his tongue polished the porringer around the rim as well as on the inside. After that he set about drying himself. In that comforting business he forgot to think any more about being drowned.

Besides being warm, it was a cheerful-looking room in other ways. There was a counter filled with bright tinny-looking teapots and sugar bowls and pitchers. The handles and spouts on these annoyed the kitten. Somehow they didn't seem to belong to the teapots, the sugar bowls and the pitchers — not as a kitten's tail, for instance, belonged to a kitten.

But on a higher shelf the kitten saw some plates and a

tankard or two which were strangely different from the ware on the counter. There was a soft glow about the dishes on the high shelf, which somehow reminded the blue kitten of the moonlight on the river the night he had listened to the river's song. And the handles on the tankards, which stood on the high shelf, did belong. The kitten stretched his neck in order to admire them.

"So, kitten, you like the pewter I fashioned in the old days, do you?" asked the man whose face was round as a pewter plate, and whose cheeks were the color of ripe apples. And the speaker, too, paused to gaze at the dishes on the high shelf.

"Well, the pewter there on the shelf was from a good formula. The master of all American pewterers gave it to me. And the molds were the best in Connecticut. But it took a long time to fashion such pewter. And there wasn't any money in it."

Pewter! Hmm! thought the kitten. This must be Ebenezer Southmayd, the pewterer! Well, my mother and the river were right. I did go through a lot, falling into the well and being two-thirds drowned, to say nothing of being four-thirds frightened to death.

But now, thank goodness, I have only to sing my song and I shall have a comfortable hearth forever. I certainly am glad I listened to the river!

He curled his long blue tail around him and sat up straight to show off his fluffy white waistcoat. Then, slowly, for he must remember each line, he began to purr.

"*Sing your own song, said the river.*"

Ebenezer Southmayd, who was mending a teapot spout

for a neighbor, laid down his soldering iron and looked over the top of his spectacles.

"Why, kitten!" he cried in amazement.

Oh, it was easy enough, this matter of getting a mortal's attention, thought the kitten, as Ebenezer Southmayd put his elbows on his knees, cupped his face in his hands, and stared at the bundle of blue by his hearth.

"*With your life fashion beauty,*" the kitten purred.

Ebenezer lifted his eyes toward the bright, tinlike dishes on the counter. "Stuff!" he said, contemptuously. "Stuff! Any country pewterer could have made *them!*" His eyes ran over the teapots with their ugly spouts, over the sugar bowls and the pitchers with the handles which didn't seem to belong to them. He sighed deeply.

"*Riches will pass and power,*" continued the kitten.

"I never had much of either," said Ebenezer.

"*Beauty remains . . .*"

The man's eyes went to the single high shelf.

"*Beauty remains . . .*" he echoed. "Yes, I knew that once, blue kitten. There are the plates and the tankards to prove it. There is the work I would not sell."

"*Sing your own song.*"

Ebenezer looked at his hands.

"*All that is worth doing, do well, said the river.*"

Ebenezer brought his gaze back to the singer.

"*Certain and round be the measure,*
Every line be graceful and true."

Really, thought the kitten. He was singing very well. He had not realized his voice was so good. He — then he ducked his head just in time.

For Ebenezer Southmayd had jumped up from his stool. He was grabbing the pitchers, the sugar bowls, the platters and bright plates from the counter and flinging them in all directions.

Without any warning, a pitcher came out of nowhere and settled down over the blue kitten's startled ears. And though both his front paws went up at once he could not budge it. He was a knight encased in armor now all right, but with no holes in his helmet through which he could peer. And with precious little air to breathe.

With thuds and thumpings he started rolling over and over, until he rolled beneath Ebenezer's feet and upset him as well. "Really!" groaned the kitten. "Really! Life in the meadow never prepared me for this!"

This, it seemed, was but the beginning. The next instant the kitten thought his head was being yanked from his body. But it was only Ebenezer freeing him from his pitcher-helmet.

Gulp, sniff, gulp! My! The air was wonderful. The kitten stretched his neck gratefully. Then as quickly he drew it back and down between his shoulders. For the man was flinging the pitcher itself on the coals of the open furnace. One moment the kitten saw the pitcher on the coals. The next, there was only a bubbling mass of metal, which grew redder and redder, hissing all the time until it disappeared.

Catsation! What if he, the blue kitten, had been thrown with the pitcher? By this time he would have been a blue coal, a puff of smoke. Really! One never dreamed of such things in a nest of dried clover, Queen Anne's lace and chickory. He wished, oh, how he wished he had never left that nest! He wished . . . Then he dodged a plate and a quart measure and leaped desperately to the back of a chair.

By this time the pewterer had seized two bright teapots from the counter. "Look at you!" he was storming, shaking a pot in either hand. "Look at your ugly spouts, your ridiculous handles! Is *that* the kind of work I was taught to do? The sort of work on which I was proud to set my touchmark? Is it, I say?

"Bah! You are the kind of teapots Arunah Hyde wanted for his Mansion House. 'Use the new formula,' he told me. 'It's cheaper. Makes a thinner metal. Then you can press it into shape quickly without bothering with the old molds.

Does away with the tiresome polishing and burnishing. Yet it makes bright stuff, like silver.'

"But it wasn't silver, blue kitten. It wasn't really pewter — not good honest pewter. It was the new cheap metal.

"Do you know what the master pewterer in Connecticut said of such metal, which he hated, blue kitten? I did not understand then what he meant, but now I understand.

> *"Silence is golden,*
> *Speech is silvern,*
> *But to say one thing*
> *And mean another*
> *Is the new and cheap metal.*

"Yet when Arunah talks to you and tells you how to make money, and make it quickly, a dark mood comes over you and you almost believe in what he is saying. So I did as Arunah wanted. But I did not put my touchmark on my work any more. I said it was because I made pewter only for the neighbors, and that using it was a waste of time. I knew all the while that my words were not true.

" 'Faster,' said Arunah, and I worked faster. My work grew more and more ugly. So I locked the touchmark away. I didn't use it — because I was ashamed. Oh, the new stuff sold right and left. Because it was new it became a fashion. But I knew it was both cheap and ugly."

The man was quiet for several minutes. He was looking straight at the blue kitten. Then in a voice so low the kitten had to bend his head and perk his left ear forward in order to hear, the man said slowly:

"Blue kitten, what a fool I have been! I, Ebenezer Southmayd, who once made pewter fit for a king."

He seemed to expect a reply, so the blue kitten nodded solemnly. He didn't understand much that had been told him. The river had spoken of kings, but the blue kitten had never met one. But the kitten did know that this man had listened to the song of the river as he, the blue kitten, had purred it, and had understood the meaning of the song. Now all that he, the blue kitten, had to do was to teach him to sing that song. Then his own troubles would be over, and he would lie in comfort on the man's warm hearth.

So the blue kitten started once again on the river's song. Over and over he sang it, while Ebenezer Southmayd moved about the shop, uttering no sound, but working quietly.

The kitten found a window ledge where the sun shone in upon him. Sometimes, being young, he went to sleep right in the midst of the song. When he woke he would take up the song where he had left off. The first time he woke from such a cat nap, Ebenezer was looking through his spectacles at a yellowed paper, and weighing some lumps of metal into an iron caldron. "Just so much of this. Just so much of that," he was saying. Then he swung the caldron over the gleaming coals.

When next the kitten opened an eye the pewterer was pouring the melted mass into two molds. Hours later, when the metal had cooled, the molds were opened and there were two hollow pieces, something like bowls, or the two halves of a ball, decided the kitten — which the man

soldered carefully together. He worked slowly and sometimes he fumbled. But at last he was turning the single
piece of pewter around and around, smoothing it on the
lathe, until the kitten drew near to watch.

Ebenezer stopped and held his work under the kitten's
nose. "Look, blue kitten, look sharp. You cannot even see
where it is joined. My hand has not lost its cunning. Now
for the top and the spout and the handle. If I succeed with
these I shall know that my eyes still retain their judgment.
This is the teapot I used to dream of doing, blue kitten.
And I shall do it yet — if I have time. If — I — have —
time!"

As he finished speaking the man began to hum. And the
blue kitten looked at him hopefully. The tune of the river
was there, in places. But only in places. And there were no
words.

So the kitten himself began to purr the river's song
again. Mortals were certainly stupid. *He* had not taken so
long to learn the song.

Ebenezer paused now and then to crumble part of a
loaf of bread into some milk that a neighbor had brought.
Yet before he was finished, he would push the bowl aside
and hasten back to his work. Then the blue kitten would
slip over and take what remained.

The man did not seem to notice the kitten at all. His
eyes were riveted on his work. But his humming was growing louder, and there was more and more of the tune of
the river's song in that humming. The movements of his
hands, the kitten noted, were certain and sure.

It was dusk when Ebenezer Southmayd called to the

blue kitten. His voice held strange excitement. "This is the dream I always had. The best piece of work I have ever done," he said.

He held the finished teapot in his hands, turning it about excitedly, peering down upon it by the light of a candle.

Even the blue kitten could see that every curve was as it should be, every line was true. Both spout and handle seemed fairly to blossom forth in grace, so perfectly were they part of the teapot itself. And the glow of the metal was as soft and lovely as the plates and the tankards which stood on the high shelf.

Ebenezer sat down on the stool, moving slowly as though very tired. He cradled the teapot in one arm, and his other hand rested for a moment on the blue kitten's head. "I am glad you came, blue kitten," he said.

Then he rose and, still moving slowly, went to a chest in the corner. Out of it he drew a strange tool. "This is my touchmark," the man said proudly.

He heated one end over the coals and pressed it on the bottom of the newly finished teapot.

The blue kitten drew near and began to weave back and forth in delight at the man's feet. His eyes were on the teapot, and his tail curved in the same shape as the handle, his neck arched like the teapot's spout.

For Ebenezer Southmayd at last was singing the song of the river. From beginning straight on to the end, he sang.

> *"Time is the mold, time the weaver, the carver.*
> *Time and the workman together.*

Sing your own song.
Sing well, said the river, *sing well."*

"Look, blue kitten," he said when he had finished. And he held the bottom of the teapot in front of the amber eyes beside him. "There is the touchmark of Ebenezer South-mayd!"

The mark was a ship under full sail. And beneath it were the initials, E.S.

"This teapot," said the man proudly, though his voice shook, and the blue cat understood that he was very tired, "this teapot is work fit for a king. For a king!"

Gently he put the pot down on the workbench, and rested his head beside it. His hand, after a moment, dropped and hung loosely at one side. The kitten placed his head against the fingers for an instant. Then, startled, the blue kitten drew back.

Ebenezer Southmayd was dead.

For a moment the river, which the kitten had not heard before, seemed to be singing loudly, as though it were in the very room. But since that could not be, the puzzled

blue kitten went to the window and looked out into the night. A mist lay over the valley, but it parted for an instant and the blue kitten thought he saw a ship passing by — a ship under full sail. Which was utter nonsense, he told himself, for how could there be a ship passing through a Vermont valley?

The neighbor who delivered the milk every evening, knocked at the door and, hearing no answer save the kitten's mewing, put his hand on the latch.

As the man entered, the blue kitten slipped past his feet and fled into the mist and damp. He was very lonely. And he had still to find a hearth for himself. That evening the blue kitten could not have said whether he was glad or sorry that he had listened to the river's song.

John Gilroy, THE WEAVER

Mr. Gilroy had a loom on which was woven the twin table-cloths. A man who knew the weaver declares that he drew some of his designs for these tablecloths from old buildings in the town.

— From an old newspaper.

CHAPTER FOUR

JOHN GILROY, THE WEAVER

Now IF I were just an ordinary kitten I wouldn't have such a time to find a hearth, thought the blue kitten, remembering what his mother had told him. But she had never told him about the three black hairs in the end of his tail, so he did not dream for an instant that he might, after all, turn out to be an ordinary cat. To be sure his mother had said this might happen and the river had suggested it. But the blue kitten felt in his very bones that he was a superior creature. So, even while he mewed plaintively his wish to be ordinary, he didn't for an instant consider such a frightful possibility.

In the morning when the mist lifted, he decided to continue straight along the way he had come. As it grew lighter he paused to look at one or two houses as a possible home. He even jumped on the window sill to peer inside what turned out to be a hatter's shop. He did want to be satisfied this time. Comfort made such a difference in a kitten's life. While if he ever lived to be old, it might mean even more.

He had come nearly to the center of the settled mile of road of which the river had told, when he saw a small house. Over the door was a swinging sign:

JOHN GILROY
WEAVER

And standing beneath that sign, with his head nearly touching it, was a tall, rather thin, man. The kitten saw that his hair was black and curly, his eyes a curious blue which turned to gray now and then. He saw too that this mortal's face was deeply lined. Suffering and sorrow, the kitten's mother had said, made such lines on mortals' faces. Sometimes they were good lines. Sometimes they were bad. The lines on this man's face, the kitten knew at once, were good lines. Even before he heard the man speaking, he felt that his chances of finding a hearth here were good too. Very good indeed.

John Gilroy was talking to two women, who stood before him. At the same time he was stroking with his long, sensitive fingers some hanks of silken white. The kitten stood beside the two women to listen.

"Good flax yarn," the weaver was saying. "The work of a whole year."

"Aye," said the older woman. "Flax sowed last May as my mother taught me."

The younger woman, who still held her yarn on one arm, smiled and her eyes took on a faraway look, so that the blue kitten gazing up at her understood she was seeing the very sowing.

The older woman went on. "I myself ran the flax through the rippling comb to shell off the seeds and soaked it in the brook by the kitchen door until it was soft. I helped with the breaking and swingling, until all the harsh part of the stalk was gone, and ran it through the hatcheling comb to take out the short fibers. Oh, this was a task. But the spinning was another matter."

Dear me, thought the blue kitten, how tiresome a woman can be. He looked at the weaver and was astonished that the man did not seem to find the woman tiresome in the least. Instead he was watching her face, as though her words were something he had hungered for.

"Another matter?" he asked as the woman paused.

"Aye. The spinning I did between heavy tasks — to rest myself." She hesitated and seemed to search for words. "There is dignity in spinning," she added.

She looked down at her hands wonderingly, as though astonished that they should have had part in fashioning the hanks of linen yarn which John Gilroy the weaver held so lightly on one arm.

"I would like to look inside your house, to see whether it pleases me," mewed the blue kitten to the weaver.

But no one paid the slightest attention. Instead, the younger woman with the far-off look in her eyes broke in suddenly:

"The fields were so lovely. Blue and then gold. Is it not a strange thing that the thread is so white? I made up a song about it to hum at my spinning.

"Here I am spinning, spinning,
White yarn my fingers yield,
Though all the while I'm spinning, spinning,
Blue flowers in a golden field."

"You bleached the flax well," praised the weaver.

"One does not throw away lightly the work of a year," said the first woman.

"Nor the beauty," added the second.

"But why," questioned the weaver, "have you come to me? You must know that I weave woolen yarn only, and spend most of my time working for Arunah Hyde. He pays very well."

"You are the best weaver in Castle Town," said the first woman. "And we want only the best."

"Besides," added the second, "you come from Ireland. All Irish weavers can weave linen yarn. Make Arunah wait."

"Aye," agreed the first, more sharply. "Make him wait."

"Wait? Arunah?" The weaver looked astonished.

"We have worked hard," reminded the first woman.

"We want to remember this year forever," said the second, very gently.

By this time the blue kitten, who felt *he* was doing the waiting, began purring the song of the river. After all, *he* had listened long enough.

"Were the fields very blue?" asked the weaver, not paying any attention to the purring at his feet.

"Blue? As the sea itself! And golden as the sands!" said the second woman. She began to hum her weaving song once more, only this time she said, *"Blue sea and golden sands."*

"Then it is fitting that the thread be as it is, as white as the surf," said the weaver. "The surf is the thread of the sea. Now, what do you want me to weave for you?"

"Tablecloths." The two women spoke together. And the first added, "Neither of us has ever had a white cloth, and a white cloth on the table does something to a house."

"There is a holiness about it — such as one feels in a church at communion time." The second nodded.

By this time the kitten was halfway through the river's song. And in the silence which followed, the purr could be heard plainly.

"Riches will pass and power. Beauty remains.
  Sing your own song."

Now that the kitten saw John Gilroy was really listening, he took full advantage.

"Out of yesterday song comes, it goes into tomorrow."

"Long ago in Ireland, I planned . . ." began the weaver.

"So, it is agreed." The second woman said nothing, but thrust her hanks of yarn on the man's other arm, which came up to receive the light burden.

Then the women turned and, with a rustle of skirts and petticoats, hurried out to the chaise by the roadside where an old brown mare had been waiting patiently. The older woman climbed in after the younger, gathered up the reins, and chirped with her lips. At the sound the old brown mare started off. The sound of the hoofs of the mare plodding along the dirt road and the creaking of the off hind wheel kept perfect time to the purring of the blue kitten, still sitting under the sign of the weaver and playing with a skein of linen yarn which brushed his nose.

"With your life fashion beauty."

"Well, I might as well — for once, pusskins," said John Gilroy, lifting the yarn out of the kitten's reach. "You have a nice purr. Come in and make yourself comfortable."

It was as easy as that. When your bones tell you that you are a superior creature you should trust them.

The kitten breakfasted, amply if not richly, on some crumbled johnny cake and bacon grease. And all the while the weaver stood stroking the linen yarn.

" 'Tis as fine as the silk I handled in Cathay, pusskins."

The kitten reached up and pricked the man's knee gently with his claw to show that he understood.

The weaver put the yarn down and took up the kitten instead. "I think I shall put into the tablecloth a certain pagoda I remember."

The kitten began to purr.

"Riches will pass and power. Beauty remains."

The weaver stroked the purring kitten's head. "Well, you are right, pusskins. The pagoda has probably been scattered to the four winds of heaven, and the ship on which I journeyed from Ireland to Cathay is lying on the corals, with mermaids sleeping in its berths and swimming in and out the portholes. And yet I have both ship and pagoda still. I can weave them into the tablecloths and keep them forever. And the women will be pleased. They are unusual women, pusskins. I think they were born with beauty and peace and content in their hearts.

"Come, let us go for a walk."

That was better. The kitten was not interested in hearing about women.

"I am to weave their tablecloths, pusskins," said the weaver as they went out the door, "so I must picture some of the things they have known and loved all their lives."

That morning John Gilroy made many drawings in Castle Town, and the kitten listened as the man worked. He waved his tail appreciatively back and forth.

"This is the old Remington tavern," said the man. "I shall put that in the cloth. Its lines are simple. Its roof is low. I have seen its like in Ireland. Men talked here of liberty and from this tavern they went forth to make their words more than words. People eating from these table-cloths and seeing the old tavern will recall the taking of Fort Ticonderoga without a shot, in the name of Jehovah and the Continental Congress. And those who know the story of Castle Town will tell then of Samuel Beach, who walked and ran sixty miles over hills and through valleys to call volunteers to this tavern. Sixty miles is a walk, puss-kins. In Massachusetts at that time a man named Revere rode through the night to rouse men to fight for liberty. But in Vermont a man walked. That too should be remem-bered."

"Mew! Mew!" agreed the blue kitten.

"Now this is the first medical school in Vermont. They say it will soon be closed. But it will be seen on the table-cloths forever."

The weaver sketched, too, the cobbler's shop and the old church on the village green.

"They are building a new church, soon," he explained. "And this building is really not at all beautiful. Yet for these women in Castle Town the old church has meant much. So it shall go in their tablecloths."

"Mew," agreed the kitten.

Then the pair of them went back to the weaver's shop.

The loom was filled with an ugly cloth of black and white mingled together. "Woolen cloth for Arunah," said the weaver. "His favorite pepper-and-salt. What a joy it will be to weave linen and forget the man."

He cut the half-woven woolen from the loom and threw the mingled mass of cloth and yarn in a pile in a corner of the room. The kitten found the pile soft and comfortable and curled down contentedly, singing his song.

After a time John Gilroy began to sing, a song which went with the pattern growing beneath his fingers, went with the sound of the treadle, the thump of the baton pressing the warp more firmly against the woof. It wasn't the song of the river — not yet. But the kitten remembered that Ebenezer Southmayd had been some time learning the song, though *he* had known it before.

> *"Thread over and under. Thread three over and under.*
> *Two over and under. Now here is the steeple*
> *For folk to remember. Forever and ever.*
> *Sing well, said the river, sing well.*
> *Linen threads crossing, the loom shuttles tossing,*
> *Knot on the wrong side, and thread pressed down firmly,*
> *Something to keep through the spring and the winter,*
> *Yesterday held in the thread of my weaving.*
> *Yesterday deep in the song of a kitten,*
> *Yesterday held by a life weaving beauty.*
> *Sing well, said the river, sing well."*

Sometimes there was a bit more from the river's song, slipped into the weaver's song, and at such times the kitten thought John Gilroy was surely learning. Yet, at other times, he seemed to have forgotten the river's song entirely. Then one morning, the kitten, who was becoming discouraged, drew a quick breath of relief. For the weaver opened his lips and began to sing, a trifle haltingly to be sure, another whole line of the river's song.

"*Out of yesterday song comes, it goes into tomorrow.*

"After these cloths are finished," the weaver promised the kitten, "I will do another. And into that one, pusskins, I shall put all the beauty, and joy of yesterday — all the dreams I once had of tomorrow."

New words came into John Gilroy's singing that morning. And there was something about the very look on the man's face that made the blue kitten certain that in a few minutes — a very few minutes — the weaver would sing loudly and joyfully the song of the river. Seeing the light growing on the man's face, he was, the kitten understood, singing straight toward that song.

> "*Here I sit weaving and weaving,*
> *The linen threads flashing away —*
> *Dunk, dunk, dunk, dunk.*
> *Here I sit weaving and dreaming*
> *From Castle Town clear to Cathay.*
> *Dunk, dunk, dunk, dunk.*"

But just as John Gilroy flung his head back, with the words, "*Sing your song . . .*" as luck, or fate, or something would have it, there was the sound of a horse being ridden hard, a gallop which stopped suddenly at a sharp order by the weaver's very door. There was the click of spurs on the doorstone, and a demanding *Rappety-rap, rappety-rap, rap-rap-rap* on the door.

The blue kitten, lying on the pile of discarded woolen cloth and yarn, held up his head. And he saw that the weaver, who was working on the last border of the second tablecloth, looked startled.

Without waiting for the door to be opened, the rider, the one who had knocked so sharply with the butt end of his riding whip, opened it himself and strode into the room. Everything about the tall newcomer was dark and harsh. His clothes, his hair, his beard, even his eyes were dark and somber. And it seemed as though a dark cloud, too, was about him, so that the very sunlight in the weaver's cottage dimmed. The kitten, who by this time felt he knew mortals very well, had never seen one such as this.

"Quick, Gilroy," said the man brusquely. "I have come for my cloth — my pepper-and-salt. You should have brought it to me and saved my time. I must have a new suit made of it at once and the tailor must hurry, for I shall wear the suit when I sign the contract for the Lightning Express."

Express? What was that? questioned the kitten to himself.

The man's breath came as fast as his words. He had thrown down the whip and now he opened and shut his hands as though wanting them to be filled with something which must be very important, the kitten judged, so agitated was the newcomer's manner.

"Quick," he demanded, "where is the cloth?"

Instinctively the kitten had inched himself beneath a fold of the discarded woolen material, so that only one amber eye looked forth. That eye however watched with astonishment as the weaver seemed to shrivel and grow smaller in the presence of the dark one. Even the lines of the weaver's face seemed to change, and the corners of his mouth grew lax. He stood in front of his loom as though to hide the weaving from the other's sight.

Why, decided the kitten, the weaver was afraid. One mortal afraid of another! But even as he came to this conclusion, he saw the weaver's hands begin to shake.

"Quick," demanded the other. "The cloth!"

"But — but," came from John Gilroy.

"Do you mean to say my order is not ready?" demanded the other. "What is that you are doing?" He had picked up the whip, and now he pointed with it toward the loom.

"I — I have been singing my own song, sir," came from the poor weaver.

"Singing your own song? What do you mean?"

"Weaving such tablecloths as will live forever. See, are they not beautiful enough for a king?"

"Stuff and nonsense!" The whip cracked in the air and the weaver quailed as though he had been struck, while the kitten thrust himself a little deeper in his hiding place, so only the merest slit of an eye watched the room.

"Prettiness will bring you little money. I will pay you double what I promised, but the pepper-and-salt must be ready in time." The dark one put his hands in his pocket and drew out gold carelessly and generously enough, flinging the coins on the woven linen.

"You work for *me*, Arunah Hyde!" he said.

Arunah Hyde, why that was one of the names on the river's list. It was the blue kitten's turn to quail. Well, he would never enter this man's door, river-list or no river-list. That was certain!

But the weaver was picking up the coins, was bending contritely before the dark Arunah. "Yes, sir," he was saying. "It shall be done." His mouth looked very weak indeed, decided the kitten. Not only were his shoulders stooped, and all his tallness gone from him, but the very lines of his face were changed. "You shall have the cloth soon, sir," he said. "I will hurry."

After Arunah Hyde had left, it was as though the darkness he had brought with him stayed behind in the weaver's cottage. At last the weaver spoke, slowly but definitely as though he were held in the dark spell of Arunah's words.

"The tablecloth I hoped to do when these were finished, was only a dream I had, a foolish dream, no doubt. Arunah says dreams are stuff and nonsense. Gold is shining and very real."

"*Sing your own song,*" began the kitten hopefully

But the weaver opened the door and set the kitten outside. "You must run along now, pusskins," he said. "I have no time for listening to you."

The blue kitten remained for a long while beneath the sign of the weaver, looking at the door shut firmly against him. He was dismayed. He was discouraged. Could it be possible, after all, that he was just an ordinary kitten?

CHAPTER FIVE

Arunah Hyde AND THE DARK SPELL

I was born and lived for many years next to the Mansion House of Arunah Hyde, the front of which was faced with marble. A fine piazza ran across the entire front, the floor of which was of large marble slabs. Very pretentious pillars supported the roof of this piazza, continuing to the second story. These, I know, were brick encased in plaster intended to give the appearance of marble. I have heard my father say when those pillars began to crumble and were dangerous to the children, "That is a sample of Arunah Hyde's building."

— From an old letter kept in the town.

CHAPTER FIVE

ARUNAH HYDE AND THE DARK SPELL

WHEN he had been with Ebenezer Southmayd and John Gilroy, the weaver, in Castle Town, the kitten had heard at different times great commotions outside. Such commotions he learned came from coaches drawn by four and even six horses. The horses were always straining at their bits, for the whip was plied unceasingly along their flanks, as the drivers, with anxious calls and even oaths, urged them forward. Faster! Faster!

Never having moved at a fast rate himself, the blue kitten could not understand. Neither his mother's teachings nor the song of the river had given him explanation for the need of haste. Cats moved quickly only to catch mice. And his mother had, he knew, neglected this part of his education.

Yet the blue kitten could understand that the hoofs of the speeding horses might well be dangerous to a kitten, even such an extraordinary kitten as he — for of course he must be extraordinary. It would be wiser, he decided, to walk at the very edge of the highway. So, not having made up his mind in the least as to where he should go to find a hearth, nor of whom he should ask admittance, he started quietly and calmly enough, along the ditch. To be sure the next name — as he remembered it — on the river's list was that of Arunah Hyde, but he had already made up his mind not to go there, river-list or no river-list.

However, before he had taken half a dozen steps, there was the sound of great commotion behind him, the clatter of a coach, the thudding of horses' hoofs, the snapping of a whip. The kitten crouched low in the ditch where a cloud of dust, a shower of pebbles, flooded over him as the first of the horses dashed by. In desperation the kitten leaped for the safety of a rock by the side of the road.

Afterward he never could tell whether he reached the rock or whether a long thin hand reaching down from the driver's seat had snatched him in mid-air. At any rate, the kitten found himself going up and up in a half circle — never had he moved so fast — and landing with a thump, breathless but unhurt, on a cushioned seat. Who? What? But a boastful voice was already answering.

"No one, I tell you, but Arunah Hyde could move fast enough to do that! Now on — " the man was roaring at the horses — "on to the Mansion House. We must cut at least three seconds from yesterday's record. Faster, fast . . ." The thin and cruel whip once more began lashing the sides of the horses.

The blue kitten looked at the roadside moving like a flash on either hand. He would have leaped but he did not dare. So he cowered, low on the seat, the dark spell of Arunah Hyde flooding over him, frightening him, even as it had frightened the weaver.

Then his memory and his hope came to his aid. Surely the river had mentioned this man. And it might be, after all, the river knew there was a hearth in Arunah's house suitable even for a blue kitten. Arunah Hyde was an important man, that was certain. Even the weaver had bowed low before him.

Just then deep, deep from the kitten's memory came a very whisper of words, words which until that moment had been quite forgotten. He had been dozing a little, the cat admitted, when the river told him of Arunah. But he had dreamed as he slept. And from that dream — or was it a dream? — came the warning. It seemed as though his left ear, even now, was twitching a little.

"Never sing your song to him!
Take heed of what I say!"

Such a memory was silly. What had he come to Castle Town for, if not to sing his song?

"Sing your own song," began the blue kitten. The purr wasn't very loud, for the blue kitten was like to sneeze from the dust. Even his teeth felt gritty.

Flash, snap, went the whip, snarling as it bit into the sleek wet sides of the horses. Flash, snap, clack, clack.

"Faster! Faster! We've but a minute to go," yelled Arunah. "There's yesterday's record — we must beat that. Beat that!" The whip slashed at the horses, and the man's eyes were on the watch set deep in a block of wood lashed on the dashboard. He must go faster. He must!

"Sing your own song," mewed the cat bravely.

"I am singing it," cried the man through clenched teeth. "Hurry! Hurry!" Up came the whip, and the kitten shuddered with the horses, while Arunah yelled.

"Castle Town shall be the center of the Universe. And I shall be the center of Castle Town!"

And before the blue kitten could catch his breath to start the second line of the river's song, the coach and six stopped before a most imposing building. The front of it shone white in the sun, for that front was fashioned of marble. Tall white columns were set along a front porch, columns which went up and up.

This was quite different from the humble quarters of Ebenezer Southmayd and John Gilroy. Even the blue kitten was impressed. He would, he decided, at least take a look at the hearth. He jumped down from the cushioned seat, and from habit hastened to test his front claws on the first white column.

Pshaw! He sneezed disdainfully, as white powder showered over him. He did not know that the column was only brick covered with plaster, and not hard like the slabs of the floor at all. He knew only there had been enough dust and sneezing for one morning.

But Arunah was swooping him up once more. "Nice kitty, nice kitty," he was saying soothingly. "Come into my mansion. You shall drink thick cream from a silver bowl, until . . ." It was a good thing, perhaps, that the blue kitten could not see the glitter in the man's eyes, the amused quirk of his mouth.

The man's voice did sound strange, but the words were words of welcome, so the kitten began stating his terms hopefully.

"And live, I hope, by a warm hearth," he mewed. Still, even as he asked for this, deep from inside his brain again came the warning — words of caution which he could not recall ever hearing. And this time there was no doubt about it, his left ear was twitching.

*"Beware of Arunah! Take heed, blue kitten.
For you work different spells."*

Arunah Hyde was putting a silver bowl — he *said* it was silver, but it was only Ebenezer Southmayd's cheap tinny metal — in front of the blue kitten. The bowl was filled with yellow cream. The cream was thick and good. The blue kitten weighed eight ounces more after drinking it. He felt changed and comfortable — and a little dull, as he sat down by the edge of a great hearth, where he was in danger of being trod on, to watch what happened next.

It was, the blue kitten soon learned, most exciting to live in the Mansion House. Rush! Rush! Rush! Through the opening door he caught glimpses of this coach and that stopping, exhausted horses with steaming nostrils, their sides wet and dripping and marked always with the whip.

The people the coaches brought streamed in through the doors. The moment they were inside, these travelers were rushed to the tables for mulled cider and brandy.

"Quick! Quick!" Arunah kept calling to the women who prepared and brought great tankards of the steaming drinks.

"Quick! Quick!" he would call to the travelers who were drinking. A horn would sound urgently after Arunah's words, and the travelers were hurried out. The whips were plied. All day long one stagecoach after another was either appearing or disappearing in clouds of dust, and travelers were streaming in and out of the Mansion House.

Arunah was here. He was there. He was ordering a horse saddled to rush the mail north, for the coach to the north was five minutes overdue. And the mail would be late.

"Late! Late!" cried Arunah, wringing his hands, almost weeping with dismay. "Late! Late!"

Arunah tumbled the blue kitten out of the rocker, for the travelers had crowded him from the hearth. Arunah brushed the kitten off a stool. He crunched his tail underfoot. Or he pushed him with one boot out of his way.

But he fed him often. Thick, yellow cream from the silver bowl that was not silver at all, though Arunah always said that it was. Tinny plates filled with delightful lake salmon, or piled high with chicken. And the blue kitten grew and grew. He gained six ounces more or less every day. His eyes glazed now and then from the abundance of food in his stomach. He was growing fat and lazy.

Arunah paused occasionally to heft him. Then one day he burst out. "My, you are almost grown, blue kitten. When you are a cat you will be fat indeed. Then you will be useful to me. Very useful."

The blue kitten did not like the sound of the words. It was almost as though they held a threat. Om — om. What was the word he had heard someone say. Ominous! That was it. Ominous! It was about time, decided the kitten, that he teach Arunah the song. He had kept putting it off because the man was so busy. And *he* had been busy too, drinking cream, eating salmon and chicken. But now that Arunah had paused for a little to admire him, he would see what he could do.

"Purr," began the blue kitten. He managed to get as far as to purr loudly about the song coming out of yesterday and going into tomorrow. Then using his most persuasive notes the blue kitten begged, "*Sing your own song,*" when Arunah, the restless, interrupted him.

"I have sung a song. And it is my own," he boasted. "No one in Castle Town, I tell you, has sung such a song, nor sung so fast, nor so loudly. For who else has done what I have done? And who will be remembered as I, Arunah Hyde, shall be remembered?

"For I came to this town a poor boy, dependent on my relations. I swept people's floors, anyone's floors. I clerked in a store. I was at everyone's bidding. But I worked. How I worked, and I went without. I saved every penny till I bought that store. I, Arunah, was the business man, the merchant. People began to bow to me then. I bought more and more. And I prospered. I had gold. I had power. I had a mill. I had a quarry. I hired carpenters and they built a school for me. People bowed still lower. I was the projector. I was the architect — or at least I furnished the money . . ."

"I, I, I," yowled the blue kitten. "Listen to *me*! I am the blue kitten, and most unusual. I . . ."

"I," answered Arunah. "I am Arunah Hyde. You are only a queer-looking kitten, growing into a queer-looking cat. You, listen to me. I shall sign the contract for the Lightning Express. There will be twice as many stages coming

and going. Then I shall put Castle Town on the map. I
shall make it the center of Vermont, of the Universe."

"I have heard that before," interrupted the kitten.

But Arunah would not listen.

"I opened streets. I built houses and stores. I built this,
the Mansion House. And listen, you kitten, to the horses'
hoofs — faster, faster, faster.

"*Horses from Sudbury, Middlebury,*
Racing to Burlington, to Woodstock
And to Hanover,
Hear the thudding of their hoofs,
Hear the snapping of the whip
Faster, faster, always faster,
Along the shore of Lake Champlain,
To Ticonderoga and Lake George,
To St. Johns and Montreal,
Hoofs flashing through Albany,
Heading for New York and city streets.
Those are my horses, those are my stages,
In Washington, men speak of me, Arunah Hyde,
I am a power, a great power I tell you,
Gold pours from my fingers,
And Castle Town is the center of the Universe,
And I, I, Arunah Hyde, am . . ."

"Mer-oww! Oww!" yowled the blue kitten who was
almost a blue cat by this time. "For pity's sake, man, stop.
I heard, or I dreamed I heard, long ago that a dark spell
was being woven about Castle Town. And now I know
that you are the one who is weaving that spell. And the

spell has mastered you. So, do stop, Arunah Hyde, for pity's sake! For your sake! For everybody's sake!"

But Arunah paid no attention. "I have mills, I say. And a quarry. I cut marble for my housefronts. I make roofs from my own slate."

"*With your hands fashion beauty,*" put in the blue kitten loudly. He was determined to be heard. After all, it was *his* song, *his* spell that was important.

"With my hands, I count gold," Arunah spoke louder.

"*Riches will pass and power. Beauty remains!*" yowled the big, fat blue kitten.

"That is nonsense. Utter nonsense," yelled Arunah.

"*All that is worth doing, do well,*" said the kitten.

"Do fast," corrected Arunah.

> "*Certain and round be the measure,*
> *Every line be graceful and true.*"

"Lines are nothing. Put on a good front," cried Arunah. "Set something new in the window, a fat blue cat, for instance. Then the travelers will pour faster into the Mansion House. *Mansion* is a good name, blue cat. For you are a cat now. *Tavern* would sound altogether too unpretentious."

> "*Time is the mold, time the weaver, the carver,*
> *Time and the workman together.*"

Never had the cat — the blue cat purred so loudly. For with cathood his voice had unexpectedly deepened. It was really magnificent. At the end of the song, he threw back his head and yowled triumphantly.

"Besides, I won't stay in the window of your old Mansion House, Arunah Hyde! Never!"

"You will if you are stuffed with sawdust!" gloated Arunah. "You are fat enough right now!" And he grabbed for the blue cat.

The cat struggled. He scratched and bit and clawed. He clawed and bit and scratched. But because he was so fat his breath was short and he was losing the fight.

When — a stagecoach came crashing to a stop. And Arunah must needs drop the blue cat to rush forward to the door. But even as he rushed he held onto the blue cat's tail.

The cat, with one final surge of strength, tore his tail loose from Arunah's grasp. And as the door opened the blue cat dashed through. Only a few hairs from his tail remained in Arunah's hands. And what were a few hairs compared to the life of a grown-up blue cat?

Away from the Mansion House dashed the blue cat. Up the road and up the road, back the way he had come. Not even Arunah's horses ever ran as hard and fast as the blue cat was running. At least he had learned speed from Arunah. He was headed back for the meadow where he was born. Past the cobbler's shop he ran, by the old tavern the weaver had sketched for his weaving, past John Gilroy's shop, to the village green and the shop where Ebenezer Southmayd, the pewterer, had worked. On and on, back and back, raced the blue cat, losing weight with every step.

When he was quite exhausted he hid under a mulberry bush and considered. Somehow, in spite of what Arunah Hyde had almost done to him — stuffing him with cream in order to stuff him with sawdust — the blue cat felt sorry for the man.

Speed and gain and power. That was Arunah's spell, and it drove Arunah Hyde harder than he drove his horses. It was a dark spell, spreading far and wide over Castle Town.

" 'And in the end that spell will overpower him.' I am sure that was what the river said, or something very like. I was asleep, or 'most asleep — but still I heard. I must have heard. Poor Arunah!" mourned the blue cat. "Poor, poor man!"

Two great crystal tears gathered and dropped slowly from his amber eyes. One was for Arunah. One was for the thick yellow cream, the beautiful lake salmon and the plates piled high with chicken, which the blue cat had left forever behind him.

A long, mournful, unearthly sound went through the valley, wailing up and down, louder, more frightening than any loon. Wailing, wailing, from Bird Mountain to Lake Bombazine.

The blue cat was startled, for he had never heard such a sound. He felt tired and sick, very sick. His thoughts began to swirl in his head, like the yellow cream swirled when poured into Arunah's tinny bowl. The sound was, he decided, a whistle of some sort from the future. Blue cats, who were born under a blue moon, his mother had said, often heard things no ordinary cat could hear.

No ordinary cat — he grew sicker and sicker. Could Arunah have poisoned him before he left? How terrible

to die of poison before he had found a hearth to fit his song!

No ordinary cat — no hearth. Oh, dear. He wished that he *was* an ordinary cat. The tip of his tail pained him a little and he remembered that he had left some of the hairs from the very end of it in Arunah's hand. He grew sicker and sicker as he lay underneath the mulberry bush. And he wished, oh, how he *wished*, that he was an ordinary cat, and not having such a difficult time to find a hearth.

An ordinary cat! It was his last thought. But the blue cat, lying with his eyes closed under the mulberry bush, did not know that with the losing of three black hairs from the end of his tail, he had lost his only chance to be an ordinary cat. Come what might he was the blue cat. And he would remain the blue cat to the end of his days. He was really most unusual. A truly extraordinary cat. He was *the Blue Cat of Castle Town!*

The Barn Cat
of Sylvanus Guernsey

It is the job of a barn cat to catch mice.
— Universal Catology.

Cat — a carnivorous quadruped which has long been kept by man in a domestic state as a pet and for catching rats and mice.
— Webster's Dictionary.

CHAPTER SIX

THE BARN CAT OF SYLVANUS GUERNSEY

THE thin blue cat woke at last. He sat up and looked weakly about him. He must have been lying under the mulberry bush for a long, long time. He must have . . . Now, let me see, he thought. What was it I was trying to do when . . . ?

But the cat could remember only that he had been going somewhere, running as fast as he could, as fast as the Lightning Express — whatever that might be.

He stirred, and though he ached in every muscle and bone, he managed to creep around to the other side of the mulberry bush. There he gazed upon a narrow lane leading off the main road and meandering over a hill. At the bend of the lane a wisp of smoke was rising from a chimney and losing itself in a riot of scarlet and gold maple leaves. The house itself could be seen in gray patches through a thinning thicket of cherry and alder. The lane seemed familiar. Perhaps, thought the cat, perhaps I was going there.

Having come to this conclusion, he stood up, crossed the road in a shaky fashion, and then slowly and painfully started up the lane. He stopped often to rest. His head and his tail hung low. As he rounded the bend, however, he lifted his head again. This time he saw a yellow tabby in the doorway of a barn next to a small, unpainted house. The tabby stopped washing her face to watch him. She was an ordinary cat, and seemed vaguely familiar. While he looked at her, she mewed in a friendly fashion. The blue cat tried to answer. But he was too weak. The gray borders of the lane — the faded goldenrod and the spilling milk-weed pods — seemed to whirl about him. The blue cat shuddered twice, then he sank down and lay still in the dust of the lane.

When next the blue cat opened his eyes, he was curled in a comfortable nest of dried clover, Queen Anne's lace and chickory, in the corner of a warm and comfortable haymow. He could hear cows in their stanchions stirring and munching at their hay. Some hens were clucking softly. A stream of sunlight coming through a little dust-covered window sifted down warmly upon him. A spider worked at her web.

Sweet fragrance from the hay rose all about. Every-thing in that place was filled with beauty and peace and content. Everything, that is, except the blue cat. His stom-ach was empty — horribly empty. One cannot see beauty or know peace, and certainly no one can be content with an empty stomach.

Just then, picking her way quietly over the haymow, came the yellow tabby with the friendly mew. From her mouth hung a nice fat mouse. The tabby hurried when she saw the blue cat's hungry eyes. With a flourish of her tail she laid the mouse down in front of him. Then, head on one side, she withdrew a bit to watch.

"Mmmm," purred the blue cat gratefully, when his stomach was mouseful and comfortable. "Mmmm, that was a breakfast fit for a king."

"I never heard of such," said the tabby cat. "But being only a barn cat, there are many things of which I never heard. If I were a blue cat, like you, matters would be quite different. Are you a king?"

The blue cat's old pride came over him and for a moment he fairly swelled with importance, although he knew no more about kings than the barn cat. Still the word, when she said it, sounded important.

"I am the blue cat," he said. "And I know the song — the song — Why! What is the song I know?"

The barn cat shook her head. "I sing my own song, the song of the hunter. I am the best mouser in Castle Town. In time I expect to catch rats!"

"*Sing your own song,*" said the blue cat wonderingly. "That is it! Or at least that is the beginning. But what about the rest of the song? And what am I to do with it?"

"Don't worry about that until you are stronger," urged the barn cat. And she mewed until the blue cat followed her to the bowl of milk in a stable corner.

"It is there every night," said the barn cat. "Sylvanus Guernsey filled the bowl last night. Tonight Zeruah, his daughter, will fill it. For every winter Sylvanus goes away. He walks all the way back to Connecticut where he works for other folk until spring. Then he returns to Castle Town and makes spinning wheels. Most folk do not buy them any more. But Sylvanus likes to make them. Zeruah will be lonely this winter, for her mother has died.

"Besides Zeruah does not like to do anything. But she will care for us creatures in the barn after a fashion, though she does not make friends with us. She does not make friends with anyone. She is not good-looking and she is certain nobody likes her."

Just then Zeruah herself lifted the latch of the barn door and came in, milking pail on her arm.

The blue cat shook his head in a startled fashion. "Mew! Mew!" Why, this was the girl on whose doorstone he had sat in his kittenhood, on the long-ago day when he had first started out to sing the song — the song . . . Oh, dear, he would never remember! And if he didn't something terrible was bound to happen, because he, the blue cat, would have failed in . . . What was it he would have failed in?

Over and over, day after day, the blue cat pondered these questions. The bright leaves fell from the trees, the last asters and goldenrod disappeared, the maples and sumac lost their brave scarlet, the bronze of the fern fronds dulled. The birds flew south.

The wind howled and moaned. Then the snow came, flake after flake, thicker and thicker, swirling in gusts, beating at the frost-covered window high in the barn, sifting in the door when Zeruah came with the milkpails.

It was cold. But the creatures were not cold. The cows chewed their cuds contentedly, there was the warm cluck-ing of hens, the friendly baa, baa of a sheep. Prowling over

the hay, in his thick fur coat, or curled in the comfortable nest, well supplied with mice by the barn cat, and bowls of milk by Zeruah, sometimes the blue cat forgot the song he had lost, forgot too that he had a mission to perform.

He would listen to the barn cat mewing her concern about Zeruah, until he, too, felt anxious about the lonely girl. This was strange, for until that winter, he had thought only about himself.

Of course he had reason to be grateful to Zeruah, he reminded himself. And even more grateful to the yellow barn cat.

"How can I ever repay you?" he asked the barn cat more than once. "I cannot catch even one mouse."

Mousing was something his mother had not taught him. It wasn't her fault, he explained. It was simply that as a kitten he had other matters to attend to.

"I see," the barn cat said politely. "What matters?"

"The matter of learning the song . . . Well, the song I have lost," explained the blue cat. And his voice held such a wailing note that the barn cat thought he must be hungry and stole off to catch another mouse.

Little by little that winter some memories came back to the blue cat. He did remember that he was looking for someone in Castle Town who would understand his song, and to whom he should teach that song. Then he would be given a hearth to sleep on. And then — something else would happen. Something important for Castle Town itself. Something in which Arunah Hyde was concerned.

And having remembered Arunah, the cat remembered Ebenezer Southmayd and John Gilroy. Little by little he put everything he recalled together. Until at last he had the story of his life, everything that is, except the song which he had once sung so proudly. The song — the song . . .

At last the cat sighed a long sigh. He could, he was positive, remember no more. He must have lost the song somewhere in Castle Town, lost it as he fled desperately from Arunah.

A ray of sunlight sifted through the little window above him. Warm sunlight with the feel of spring about it. In another corner of the mow two yellow kittens called to their mother. The blue cat stalked over to look at them. They were round yellow balls with perky ears and pointed tails, and they looked much like the barn cat.

"Nice enough, as kittens go," decided the blue cat, not realizing he had spoken aloud.

"Nice enough?" echoed the barn cat, leaping unexpectedly from the rafters, and pushing the blue cat aside. "Why these are the most wonderful kittens in all Vermont!"

"Hmm!" answered the blue cat, moving away. And this time, strictly under his breath, he said, "What poor judgment you have, barn cat."

He went off by himself to the farthest mow, and lay down blinking, and a little lonely. And here the ray of sun sought him out.

The sun did have a feel of spring about it. And when spring came how could a blue cat stay placidly in a barn? Besides, he would soon be too great a burden for the barn cat. How could she expect to catch mice for four? His own mother, he recalled, had thought it difficult to catch mice for two.

Once the blue cat made up his mind, there was — as his mother could have told you — no changing it. So he went immediately to tell the barn cat of his decision. "It is not spring yet, but it will be soon," he said. "And I think I had better get an early start. I have, as you know, a great many matters to attend to." He thanked her then for all she had done. "Sometime," he insisted, "I will repay you. And the girl Zeruah, as well."

"But where," asked the barn cat, "are you going? And what will you do?"

"I am going back the way I came," he told her. "To search for the song. It must be lying under the snow somewhere in Castle Town. And if I search hard enough I shall find it. I feel *that* in my bones."

"Well, after all, you are not a blue cat for nothing," answered the barn cat.

The blue cat bowed his head. Somehow the words filled him with sadness. He said, humbly enough, for he had learned a great deal, "I am blue I know. But I have decided that I am only an ordinary cat, and not even a poor mouser. Still, wherever it is lying, I must find and sing my own song. Of that I feel certain."

The barn cat hovered about him. She straightened his whiskers and even washed his ears. "Pink ears," she insisted, "are so becoming to a blue cat!"

She looked at his fine, long, white whiskers, and at the eyebrows which were like small fountains above his amber eyes. She approved the softness and whiteness of his waistcoat. That was the result of a good winter diet of mouse and milk. Then she looked him over from head to tail.

"There isn't a black hair on you," she said musingly — having with her own motherhood inherited the wisdom of all mother cats. "You certainly are an extraordinary cat!"

Then the blue cat, who didn't for an instant believe these words — remembering, for one thing, the barn cat's opinion of the yellow kittens — climbed slowly down the haymow to the floor and hurried past some hens scratching in the straw to the stable door. There he pushed open the swinging round of the cat-hole, and stepped out into the snow.

It was deeper than he thought. He lifted one foot gingerly and looked about. Snow, snow, snow, as far as he could see. Even the sun felt different here than it had in the barn. There was no least feel of spring about it now. And there was a wind which pierced like an icicle through his blue fur. Hmm! Brrrr! He set down his lifted foot and turned about to re-enter the cat-hole.

But — there was the barn cat, head and shoulders filling the round. She was looking at him proudly. "I came to see you off," she said. "And to wish you luck. Only a blue cat would dare depart in this weather."

"Thank you. Thank you very much." The blue cat spoke a trifle stiffly. Whether it was from pride or cold, he could not have said.

"I do hope you find that song," said the barn cat.

"Err — the song. Yes, I must find the song," answered the blue cat with a shiver. And he started off carefully in the path Zeruah had made. He did not look back again

until he had followed the snowy lane down to the road. From there he did look back. But all he saw were his own tracks in the snow. They made a lonely, meandering trail.

But along the road, the sleigh runners had smoothed a hard and even path, so he found the going much easier. And the sun did feel warmer. After a bit he even found himself purring hopefully. It was good to be on the way to Castle Town. There surely he would find the song. Then his special task would be to discover the mortal who would learn it. Perhaps every cat had a special task. Being, as he had definitely decided, only an ordinary cat, he could not be certain of this. But no matter. *He* had such a task. He felt it in his bones!

CHAPTER SEVEN

Thomas Royal Dake,
THE CARPENTER

I remember Thomas Dake, a carpenter in our town. He it was who cut the wood and built the new church on the green. That church was built by the Building Committee's orders more or less after the fashion of the old church. But Thomas Dake himself insisted that he should build the pulpit as he saw fit. He spent much time and thought over the arched recess and the keystone, and yet longer time over the pulpit itself, feeling that this was to be the best work of his life. When the money which he had been paid to build the pulpit was not sufficient, Mr. Dake used his own meager savings to complete the task.

— A memory of an old resident, set down
long since by a woman in the town.

CHAPTER SEVEN

THOMAS ROYAL DAKE, THE CARPENTER

So ALONG the wind-swept, snow-filled road, the blue cat came back to Castle Town, seeking the song he had lost.

But, hunt as he would in every snow bank, bending one ear and then the other earthward, he could find no trace, no least echo of that which he sought. It had frozen hard in the ground, and if he did not find it before it was too late, it would melt with the snow. It would disappear into the earth itself, to nourish the grass and the flowers, perchance the very weeds of Castle Town.

As the blue cat stalked desperately up one side of the road and down the other, he heard men and women in that town talking excitedly of Arunah Hyde, and telling one another how wonderful it would be to have Castle Town the center of the Universe.

"You will see, under Arunah's planning, there will be excitement every minute. Stages rushing in — more and more of them, filled with important people, and plenty of gold and power for all of us."

"There will be a big bank and I shall become trustee," gloated one.

"Trustee! Pah, I shall become Senator of Vermont. Later

I shall go to Washington and press laws through Congress which will make Arunah, and all of us, still richer," said another.

"I," said a third, "shall build the most showy house in the valley. It will have tall pillars like Arunah's Mansion House. Only *my* house will outshine every other."

"By jub," added a fourth. "Houses are nothing. I shall count hill after hill white with sheep. And meadows red with cattle. And all the sheep and the cattle shall be mine! Mine!"

Gold and power and possessions. And the sound of Arunah's song swelling louder and louder, a loud song echoing from one end of Castle Town to the other. While an unnoticed, lean and hungry cat searched in vain.

"I, too, had a song — once," mewed the blue cat. But no one listened to that mew. There were other and more exciting matters to attend to.

At last came a day when the blue cat lost all hope of finding the song. He came and sat on the stones at the edge of the well in the village green. The green itself was still snow-covered, but the well was fed by deep springs which never froze, and the stones at its edge were bare and warmed a bit by the sun. The cat was grateful even for the warmth of those stones.

He did not look over the edge of the well to admire himself. He did not admire himself in his own mind. He sat there and thought.

He had lost the song. He had failed in the quest. He had left his task uncompleted. It was a sad, sad time. And the blue cat was not only sad. He was quite ashamed. He wove

a little silence about himself and stayed still in the center of that silence.

Behind him a new church stood on the village green. During his search through Castle Town he had noticed day after day workmen passing in and out. The sound of the hammer and saw had been comforting. After a time the number of workmen decreased. This day only a single man had come early and entered the church. After he entered no sound of hammer or saw came forth. Only a great silence filled the church, and this at length crept out, down the steps and over the village green to the well. There it folded up and put away the little silence with which the blue cat had surrounded himself.

The blue cat felt a prickling from his ears to his paws and tail, for he had never known such a great silence. He was, being a blue cat, still curious about all manner of things, so he decided he must find out for himself what was happening inside that church. He scrooched low, his belly almost touching the snow, and crept like a blue shadow over the village green, closer and closer.

At the steps one by one his paws came up. He was on the first step. Then the second. And the third. Until — he was on the church portico — was slipping beneath the tall columns of wood, newly painted and shining white — through the little vestibule.

The great silence held. One cat's nose, one amber eye, one pink-lined ear moved slowly around a door. And then the whole of the blue cat's head.

He saw the man who had entered alone sitting in the front pew. That pew faced a great and empty arch, an arch which the cat saw later was centered between two doors, in one of which he was now standing. The man was looking at the empty arch.

The blue cat came into the church and looked at the arch too, though he saw nothing but empty space. Yet, as he watched, the man began bending his head this way and that. There were questioning lines on his forehead. His brown eyes — the color of a new plowed field — questioned, and even his lips were puckered. Every now and then he lifted his hand — roughened and worn by work — and ran it back and forth through brown hair that had ripples in it — *ripples like the river* — thought the cat. The cat's tail waved with pleasure as he thought of the word "river." But that was all. No further memories followed the word.

"Mew?" said the cat. The mew was a question.

The man looked down and smiled. It had been a long time since anyone had smiled at the blue cat. The cat responded instantly. He drew himself into a ball and jumped as lightly as a feather to the man's knee. There he too turned and looked at the arch. Then he looked back at the puzzled face above him. "Mew?" he asked once more.

The man laid his hand on the cat's head. "I am trying to see the pulpit I shall build there, blue cat," he explained. "But what kind of pulpit can I build for two hundred and fifty dollars? Not that much really. For there's my pay to come out, a dollar and a half for every day."

Money again, thought the blue cat. Just like Arunah! But only a dollar and a half a day. The man hasn't learned much. Arunah talked of thousands, and never mentioned anything less than gold.

Man and cat continued to sit on the front pew, the man still staring at the archway, the cat staring first at the archway and then at the man. And all at once the questioning lines disappeared as by magic from the man's face, and a quiet happiness came there instead. His eyes were alive at something which he alone could see. His mouth broke into a smile of pleasure. The blue cat was impressed. Perhaps, here in the silence, he would find something kindred to what the man beside him had found. Perhaps here he would find the song he had lost.

But in a trice the mighty silence was torn asunder. In tatters it lay on the floor. Then it was gone like the song which the blue cat had lost in the autumn. There was a stamping of feet on the steps, a kicking of boots against the door jamb to remove the snow, a clearing of throats and a shuffling in the vestibule. And through the other door — the one the cat had not used — came four men.

"Ah," said the man on the front pew. "The Building Committee!" And under his breath, "What a help they will be!" Slowly he stood up. It was clear to the cat that the man was not at all eager to see the visitors. Observing this, the cat at once took his stand beside him.

"We would like to have the church finished," said one who walked ahead of the others. The cat had seen the speaker often enough with Arunah.

"Have you decided," he went on, "how you will build the pulpit?"

The rest of the Committee nodded and frowned at the empty space. The man to whom he spoke hesitated.

The speaker saw the cat at this moment, and would have clouted him with his cane. But the man beside the cat stepped quickly in front of his small companion.

"This is God's house. The cat is God's creature," he said.

"More likely the devil's."

"There *are* dark goings-on in Castle Town. In this, at least, we are agreed." And as though echoing the words, there was the sound of one of Arunah's stages dashing by. Above the jingle of harness bells sounded the oaths of the driver, the crashing of his whip, a single terrified scream of a horse as the lash bit his frosted skin. That scream filled the empty church, clashing against the eardrums. The Building Committee looked at the ceiling or out the windows at the bare branches against the sullen winter sky. Not one man looked at another. The eyes of everyone were afraid.

When the last sound was gone the Committee turned to stare at the empty arch. "Come, Dake, make up your mind," urged the one who had spoken first.

"I have been thinking quietly this morning," said the man called Dake, lifting his eyes to the arch. "And I have decided I would like to make the most beautiful pulpit in all Vermont for this church. For a moment I could see how beautiful that pulpit could be — the very peace of a forest set in a church. White pine, of course, for the pulpit, first growth, clear. With rails of wild black cherry, seasoned well and polished, sweeping . . ."

"Such a pulpit will cost more money, I know." The cat noticed for the first time that the speaker, having laid down his cane, kept opening and closing his hands in the same clutching fashion that Arunah had used so much. "Always more money. We have spent altogether too much on this church already. Far more than we planned."

"It is the House of God," said the workman.

"There should be reason and economy in all things," declared the other.

"Yes! Yes! Reason and economy! Especially economy!" echoed the rest of the Building Committee.

"But such a pulpit as I am thinking of would not only be beautiful. It would fill you with peace and content every Sunday. It would keep a man humble, and would help him face sorrow and death. It would lift his soul on wings to God himself."

"You talk like a minister, Thomas Dake," said the man whom the cat had seen so often with Arunah. "You should remember you are *only a carpenter.*"

The blue cat blinked, as the words echoed in his memory. "*Only a carpenter!*" Why, it was a carpenter to whom he must go. It had something to do with the song — the song he had lost. He blinked again with discouragement. For his memory still refused to serve him.

"You should not presume to tell the Committee how to build its church, or how much to pay for its pulpit," warned the man with the clutching hands.

"I have built the rest of the church as the Committee wanted it," answered the man who was only a carpenter. "The design is in some ways overmuch like the old one, where the quarreling and bickering in this town began. And where economies toward God began too. So that the old church soon began falling to pieces and was from the first unsafe.

"This church has been built well and strong. I myself chose the very trees to go into its framework and helped to fell them. The walls stand, and will stand, four square to Heaven.

"Can I not," the carpenter was almost pleading, "can I not make this pulpit as it should be made? Make it perfect to the glory of God?"

"Certainly, if you do not spend more than two hundred and fifty."

"You agreed to do it for that, you know."

"If you can't make a profit for yourself, that is not the Committee's fault."

The words came thick and fast from one and another. "You might," said the man who was much with Arunah, "you might skimp more on material. Brown paint, for instance, instead of polished wood. What's the difference?"

"Or put in longer days."

"Or . . ."

"Never mind," said the carpenter. "I'll work it out." As he spoke the cat blinked. For the carpenter seemed to grow taller and more commanding. Even the Committee sensed the change.

The first speaker put in meekly. "Yes, Mr. Dake." His clutching hands fell listless and hung open at his sides. One of the others picked up his cane. Mufflers were wrapped about scrawny necks, coats were buttoned tightly.

The Committee departed. But the great silence which had drawn the cat in the first place was no longer in the church.

"Let's go home." It was the first time the blue cat had ever received such an invitation. Small wonder he trotted out proudly at the carpenter's heels. He forgot about being tired and hungry. He forgot for a little his grief and dismay over the song he had lost. He thought only of the words, "Let's go home."

Along Castle Town's wide street, where the snow still sparkled in the late winter sun, they went to the middle of the town. And then along a side road leading south. Just as the cat was getting a trifle wobbly, the carpenter stooped and lifted him in his arms. He cradled him comfortably there, as though he was accustomed to holding children.

They stopped at length where a white picket fence with arched gates framed a snow-covered yard, patterned with footprints. In the center of that yard was a house. It was a simple house, with a white portico over its low steps, but the portico repeated exactly the line of the three arches over the gates in the white fence. The carpenter stroked the cat. "This is the home of my Sally," he said. "I made it beautiful for her." And suddenly the blue cat saw that the house with its welcoming portico was beautiful, so beautiful that even he felt a deep satisfaction just from looking at it.

Then the door opened and Sally was framed there — Sally with a light in her eyes and welcome on her lips, a flock of children dancing about her. The color of Sally's dress matched the blue of her eyes. Her hair was the color of the sun. There were mischievous tendrils curling in a fine mist about her face, but the rest of her hair was drawn back smoothly and lay in a twisted knot at her neck. Her apron was fresh and white, and in her hand was a wisp of sewing, white like the apron.

"Sally," exclaimed the carpenter, "I had to come home to talk to you."

Sally gestured to the children, and with a whoop they were off to the brookside. Here the waters had broken through their winter covering and sang a new song of freedom as they hurried along.

The cat was deposited neatly on the steps, where he watched the two people before him, his ears bent forward to catch every word.

"Hear the brook," said the carpenter. "It was never so

loud. And look at the meadow." He gestured toward the rising land across the road from the house. There the snow had been blown or had sifted away and brown patches of earth were already showing promise of green. Upward the meadow swept, slowly losing itself in the blue-shadowed hills.

"Did God cheat when he made that meadow, Sally?" he asked. "Did He count cost in fashioning those hills? Did He use second-rate materials and work fewer hours? Did He?"

Sally looked puzzled. Then her brow cleared. "God is not mocked, Thomas Royal."

The blue cat flicked his tail as he recognized the name which the river had uttered. "His father insisted on Royal. That," said the river, "is a term applied to kings."

"Why did you call me Royal?" asked the carpenter.

"It is your name. When you have that look in your eyes, I must call you so." Sally waited quietly for a moment, her eyes on her husband's face. "I would not love you so much, Thomas Royal," she said, "did I not know that you always live up to the name."

Long after Sally had gone into the house, and the children had disappeared around a bend of the brook, the blue cat sat with Thomas Royal Dake on the stone steps under the portico.

The man's eyes were on the meadow sloping upward. But the cat knew he was seeing, not the meadow, but the empty arch in the church. At length his brows cleared. There was a deep gentleness in his eyes, and the cat knew he was thinking too of Sally.

Slowly, hesitantly the man began to sing. Then more and more confidently. The sound of the waters slipping beneath the snow was there, the triumph of the brook freed from its winter prison, the lifting slope of the meadow, the everlasting strength of the hills.

"Sing your own song, said the river,
Sing your own song.

"Out of yesterday song comes.
It goes into tomorrow,
Sing your own song.

"With your life fashion beauty,
This too is the song.
Riches will pass and power. Beauty remains.
Sing your own song.

"All that is worth doing, do well, said the river.
Sing your own song.
Certain and round be the measure,
Every line be graceful and true.
Time is the mold, time the weaver, the carver,
Time and the workman together,
Sing your own song.

"Sing well, said the river. Sing well."

And the blue cat, sitting tall and straight beside the carpenter on the steps beneath the portico, felt the song slipping into his ears, along his backbone and tingling even the tips of his paws and the end of his tail — the tail where every single hair was blue!

The cat heard the song and felt the song in the depth of his being. Then his heart answered, and suddenly the cat realized what had happened. *Here was the song he had lost!*

Here from the carpenter's lips was lifting the song of the river, the ancient song of creation which was as old as the world itself. For the Creator of All Things was the first to sing it. This was the song which he, the blue cat, must sing until he found a mortal who would not only listen but would sing it also.

Here was one who must have been born knowing the river's song, who could sing it and sing it well! The cat stared in amazement at the carpenter.

Then why? But suddenly the blue cat remembered why. Only a *blue cat* could teach that song to others. Occasionally a mortal *knew* the song, but only a blue cat could teach it. This then was the quest upon which he had been sent! This was the task which was his to do! This was the song he must sing!

The cat was almost frantic with delight. He curled and uncurled his claws. He stretched himself from head to tail. He arched his back until it was the shape of the middle arch above him. And when the carpenter began the song again, the cat sang it with him, sang it loudly and triumphantly, until Sally drawn by the sound came to the door.

"Sally," cried the man. "I shall build the pulpit. I must build it."

"Of course," said Sally.

"There will be no wages while I work on it."

"I can manage. We shall be having the garden soon."

"There is more than that." The man paused and swallowed hard. "I must use our savings, too. That troubles me. For when the new baby comes, you may have need of it. And it is not too much, as you know."

"I shall be happier if you use it. Somehow, Thomas Royal, it seems to me that the building of this pulpit is something you must do. It is a task for which you have been preparing all your life. It is like a song which must be sung. What is money compared to . . ."

"Beauty," supplied the carpenter.

"Yes," said Sally. "And peace."

"And content," purred the cat. Beauty and peace and content. Of such was the Bright Enchantment. And he, the blue cat, would have his part in bringing that enchantment to Castle Town. *He had found his song!* More than that, he believed now in that song!

Yet he did not start forth on his quest right away. Day after day he went with the carpenter to the church. There the cat lay on the front pew and watched and listened. The man sang or whistled as he worked. And the blue cat purred and purred. He was determined to relearn the song of the river so well that no matter what happened he would never forget it. Never!

Finally the day arrived when the pulpit was finished. The carpenter smoothed the last bit of simple carving, painted the last inch of the pine into whiteness, repolished the sweep of the dark shining cherry rails on either side.

He came then and took his seat on the front pew beside the cat.

"I have sung my own song, at last," said the man. "My song and Sally's. And the peace of the forest is here. It is the most beautiful pulpit in all Vermont. It is fit for the King of Kings."

The carpenter closed his eyes, but the cat looking closely saw that his lips were moving. The cat folded one paw over the other and made ready to nap. His left ear caught a whispering sound and he blinked. Then both amber eyes were wide.

Up from the simple lines of the pulpit sprang tall pines. Their branches of dark needles filled the arch and overflowed into the church, whispering, whispering. And a glory was in those pine branches. A glory and an everlasting radiance.

And to the scent of pine was added a new fragrance. From the shining polished rails grew wild cherry trees, slender and lovely, bursting into bloom beneath the sheltering branches of pine. And the sound of the singing of birds was there.

The carpenter's eyes remained closed, his lips still moving. The blue cat knew he must look no more. Softly he slipped from the pew, and bending his head reverently, he took his leave.

It was time now to finish his quest; time to carry out the task which had been his from the beginning. Time for his song to be sung.

But he would never forget the glory and the everlasting radiance.

CHAPTER EIGHT
Zeruah Guernsey, THE GIRL

*Beginning at the beginning, Zeruah Higley Guernsey
made a carpet . . . She began at the wool on the back
of a sheep . . . From sheep to carpet all the work was
done in her own home. Her father made the spinning
wheel to spin the wool. He made the wooden needle with
which she worked her designs.*

> — From the story of the carpet by
> Mary Gerrish Higley, who kept
> careful record of the things which
> happened.

CHAPTER EIGHT

ZERUAH GUERNSEY, THE GIRL

THERE was no least doubt in the blue cat's mind as to where he should go. Through the vestibule he hurried, under the white columns, down the steps and across the village green. Past Ebenezer Southmayd's shop, he went, back along the main road, until he came to a certain mulberry bush. There was the narrow lane, leading off the main road and meandering over a hill. The blue cat hurried up the lane.

The barn cat was as usual in the barn door. But this time she was washing the faces of her two kittens.

The blue cat had started toward Zeruah's doorstone, but the barn cat hailed him. "Do come and look at these kittens," she said. "They grow more marvelous every day."

"Hmm," said the blue cat, nodding wisely. Then he changed the subject. "I don't know yet just how I am going to repay you for what you did for me last winter," he began.

At the words the barn cat dashed away, for she had been reminded of something. In a whisk of a cat's tail she was back, bringing a fat mouse, which she presented with her best company manner. The blue cat was not hungry, but he ate politely.

Then he inquired about the girl, Zeruah.

"Unhappy as ever," said the barn cat. "Perhaps she is lonely for her father, who is staying a long time in Connecticut. Though I think she would be just as unhappy if he were at home. I am more worried than ever about her. She does not even tend her mother's garden."

"Perhaps," said the blue cat, "I can do something for Zeruah now. I have, you see, found the song."

"Mew!" It was the barn cat's turn to be polite.

Then, as the blue cat hurried off toward the doorstone of Zeruah's house, the barn cat, with a kitten on either side, sat and watched. This time the blue cat did not demand that the door be opened. He stretched himself in the sun on the doorstone and waited for the girl to come out. He had much to think about. Besides he had learned to bide his time.

At length Zeruah did open the door. She had a bucket on her arm, which she must go to the spring to fill. The room behind her, the cat saw, was as barren and as carelessly kept as ever. Even the girl did not look overly tidy at the moment.

Nevertheless, the blue cat stood up and began his song.

"Go away," said the girl, turning down the path in the direction of the spring.

The blue cat only purred the louder as he followed at her heels.

The girl pretended not to hear. Still the cat kept purring. And, when Zeruah bent to dip her bucket in the spring, the cat drew close and purred into her left ear. His left ear, he remembered, had always heard more than his right one.

But Zeruah paid no attention. Unless the frown between her eyes, the firm set of her chin, showed that she heard.

Oh, my dear, thought the blue cat. And he was so sorry for Zeruah that he rubbed his head gently against her hair, purring softly. There was something like a sob from the girl. At this, the cat raised his paw and rested it on her shoulder.

With no warning whatever, Zeruah loosened her hold of the bucket and flung herself face down in the grass. "I am so lonely," she sobbed harshly. "So lonely. And I am so ugly. No one will ever look at me, blue cat."

The blue cat's pink nose was at Zeruah's ear.

"*With your hands fashion beauty.*"

"If I had someone to love, I could do that, blue cat. But it is no use."

"*Certain and true be the measure.*"

Zeruah sat up and leaned her back against a pine. The blue cat crept into her lap and kept singing, low and comfortingly. He had been through so much, and had grown so discouraged, so sad, so disgusted with himself, that he could understand how Zeruah felt. It was the worst thing in the world to lose faith with oneself.

While the pine branches above whispered on and on, as though keeping time to the blue cat's song.

When Zeruah went back to the house, the blue cat followed. This time the girl did not close the door, and the blue cat walked in and made himself at home.

Day after day the blue cat sat on the uncomfortable hearth, beside the fire that smoked and smoldered and, more often than not, went out. And he sang and sang to the girl, Zeruah.

Hour after hour she sat in a straight chair, staring out of the window, seeing nothing, hearing nothing, doing nothing. Though after a time the blue cat was hopeful that her left ear did catch hungrily at the words of his song. At any rate, singing was the only thing he could do and he knew but one song.

So he sang the song of the river. Sang as he never had sung before, for he thought of Thomas Royal Dake, the carpenter, and of the understanding of his Sally. He thought of the Bright Enchantment.

If Zeruah would only learn his song, then the blue cat was certain, he could teach it to almost anyone in all Castle Town! Even if he spent every one of his nine lives trying, he was willing to spend them. For the dark spell of Arunah, about which he had heard so much that spring, and with which he, himself, was familiar, must be broken.

The blue cat had entirely forgotten that if he taught a

mortal to sing, he would find a hearth. What should happen to him no longer seemed important. The Song was important!

No wonder the blue cat's purr was a mighty purr to hear.

And then, one day, the girl put her head down on the bare table. There were tears again, but they were restful tears.

And again the blue cat was at the girl's left ear. For it was only one leap from the floor to the tabletop.

"Sing your own song."

Zeruah moved her head, in a half shake.

"Out of yesterday song comes. It goes into tomorrow."

"There has been no song for me ever," cried Zeruah. "No song in yesterday and there will be none in tomorrow."

"With your life fashion beauty," went on the cat bravely, thinking of Ebenezer Southmayd and John Gilroy, though he was astonished at the bitterness in the girl's tone.

"Fashion beauty! Hmm," said the girl. "One does not have to be beautiful to do that!"

"Sing your own song."

But Zeruah stood up. "Why should I sing? There is no one to hear," she said. "No one."

And she wouldn't, and she didn't sing. But she did listen to the blue cat.

So, over and over and over, the blue cat sang the song of the river. He sat by the uncomfortable hearth in the barren room and sang it. He sang and believed in the song.

Until at last the girl looked at the cat one morning and asked, "How can I fashion beauty?" She gave the cat no time to reply, but went on speaking as though she had been thinking about the matter for some time. "I have nothing with which to do such a thing. Nothing! I have only a sheep which my father gave me long ago. The sheep's wool is mine. When my mother was living she made me card and spin it, though I had no joy in the doing of it. There is plenty of woolen yarn! Woolen yarn! Linen would be better. I have heard that the weaver made beautiful white cloths with pictures on them. Blue cat, I wonder . . ."

Her father came home from Connecticut. On Sunday he went to the church on the village green. Zeruah would not go with him, because she was too unhappy.

When her father came home from church he told her of the pulpit. "It is beautiful," he said.

"Was it sent here from away? Did a great artist fashion it? Is it made of far-off expensive woods brought by the sailing ships?"

"Why, Zeruah, my daughter, the carpenter Thomas Dake made it. He cut the pines himself, in the grove behind our very house. And the wild black cherry from its edge."

"I will go and see this pulpit," said the girl. And she did on a week-day morning, while the cat followed at her heels. This time the cat saw nothing unusual about the pulpit. But the girl sniffed and said, "Strange I can smell pine needles and cherry blossoms."

When they came out of the church, the cat went over

in front of Ebenezer Southmayd's shop and the girl followed. Still in the window sat the teapot, the last and the most beautiful piece of work which the pewterer had fashioned.

The girl did not go to see the tablecloths but she thought about them a good deal. And she remembered the odor of pine and of cherry blossoms.

One morning Zeruah said to the cat, "Let us go to the grove behind the house."

"Purr," agreed the blue cat.

Into the shady grove beneath the tall white pines they went. And it was still save for the whisper, whisper of the pines and the purr of the blue cat. And one day as they sat together on the brown needles a silence began to weave itself about Zeruah. The cat felt a prickling — a little prickling from his ears to his paws and his tail. For the silence was like the silence which had surrounded the carpenter on the day when the cat had crept into the church and found him dreaming of the pulpit he could make.

The blue cat did not purr. He did not move. He just waited.

"Perhaps," said Zeruah to the silence. Then, "I will try."

"Could you make me a frame?" she asked her father that evening when he came from the barn. "A frame on which I could embroider — a carpet?"

As her father looked at her, she explained. "I want to use up the woolen yarn I have from my sheep. I saw a flower in the woods which I would like to keep forever. It was one which my mother used to search for."

The blue cat waited anxiously for the answer.

"The flower was in the woods where the carpenter got his trees for the pulpit," said the girl. "There are herbs and plants there I can use for dyes."

"And your other designs?"

The girl's face was beginning to glow. "From the woods, some of them. And I shall tend my mother's garden again. There is a root of the rose there which her grandmother brought from Connecticut. When it blossoms I shall put the blooms in her blue-and-white dish and put that in my carpet. I shall gather the blue flowers from the flax meadow, and I shall put these in the pewter bowl which Ebenezer Southmayd fashioned in Connecticut. It has his touchmark on it. Though I must make the bowl in colors, for there can be no thread of silver — not even from the dyes of all the plants in the woods."

"I wish you would put my white rooster in your carpet," said her father.

"The white rooster! Do you think he is pretty?"

"He is pretty to me."

Zeruah smiled gently, and the cat stared at her in amazement. She did not look plain in the least when she smiled.

"I shall put the rooster in the carpet," she promised. "But first I must tidy the house. I cannot make a carpet in a room which looks like this."

So she did. She swept the house, and brushed a cobweb from the corner. She dusted the spinning wheel and set it by the hearth. She found a cover for the table. And she put the pewter dish in the center and placed some apples in it. The blue-and-white bowl she set in the window, and put pink ragged robin and blue lupine in it.

She built up the fire so that it crackled cheerfully, while the teapot on the crane above bubbled and sang. The cat, too, sang on the bare hearth until, one day, Zeruah brought a rug, a thin rug to be sure, with nothing beautiful about it, and placed it there for him.

It was a trifle more comfortable and the blue cat was grateful as he curled himself upon it and sang his song of the river, while Zeruah took her wools and sat herself down in front of the tambour frame, with her new wooden needle in her hand.

One day Zeruah looked up from her frame. "In time, blue cat," she said, "this house will be beautiful. I can almost see the carpet on the floor. And when the carpet is finished . . ." She paused and looked calculatingly at the blue cat.

"Blue cat," she said, in a curious musing tone. "Blue cat, I am going to keep you forever."

The cat, who had been lying peacefully on the hearth rug, arched himself in the air and turned completely over, as though a hot coal had struck him. He remembered Arunah's promise to keep him forever. Arunah had planned to stuff him with sawdust. And now — Zeruah. Why, Zeruah was saying the same thing! He sat up straight and glared at her.

But the girl was laughing aloud. "Oh, blue cat," she said. "You have done so much for me with your singing. So I shall put you in my carpet, just as you looked now, blue cat. Glare and all. You, sitting there on your ugly rug! For even with the glare you are not ugly to me, blue cat. You see, I love you."

And suddenly Zeruah began singing the song of the river.

The blue cat relaxed. He lay down once more and listened. He felt a mighty satisfaction because he had carried out his quest. He had taught a mortal to sing the song of the river.

He felt a little sad too, for he had promised himself to do even more. If Zeruah learned the song from him, then he had promised himself to teach others in the valley. And that meant he must leave the room which he had grown to love. He must . . . Wait! There was something else he must do first. He must find a way to thank the barn cat for what she had done when he had been tired and sick and discouraged. *That* would require some thinking.

Compared to the song of the river, a thank-you for the barn cat should have been a simple thing. But for a long time the blue cat could not think of anything suitable. She was the best mouser in Castle Town. He could catch grasshoppers, but she did not care for them. And birds were beyond his ability. So what could he — a blue cat — do for one as capable and competent in every way as the barn cat had shown herself to be? And who was, in her opinion at least, the mother of two most remarkable kittens.

Then, one day, Zeruah called to the blue cat. "Come and see yourself," she said, as she lifted him to the chair in front of the tambour frame. "You really are a remarkable cat!"

There, looking back at him from the frame, was his own blue self — the self he remembered from the brief glimpse he had taken so long ago in the well on the village green. Older, of course, with the marks of a difficult life behind him. But with his white whiskers standing out straight and well kept, above his white waistcoat. As he gazed, and almost felt like yowling and spitting at the creature before him — so like it was to himself, he knew what he could do for the barn cat.

Straight to the barn he went and brought in the yellow kittens one at a time and placed them on the striped rug on the hearth. The barn kittens were pretty big by now, and a load, but the blue cat managed.

Plain as plain his mew said to Zeruah, "Put them in the carpet too. They are remarkable kittens. Or so their mother thinks!"

So Zeruah did.

And the barn cat was pleased. "Only a blue cat," she said, "would have recognized how remarkable those kittens really are."

The blue cat held his peace, as a gentleman and a blue cat should.

But the story of the carpet, which Zeruah was making, spread through the town. And report of the pictures of the blue cat and the yellow kittens spread likewise.

"Spitting likenesses, I tell you!"

The curious from Castle Town came to see this wonder. And when they saw the neat house which Zeruah kept, and the beauty of the carpet growing beneath her fingers, to say nothing of the bright happiness of the girl's face, those who came envied her. And they, too, wanted to do something with their hands.

Zeruah helped them plan things they could make, beautiful things. Some were simple like pot-holders and knitted lace and canes with curious handles. And some were difficult like coverlets and bedspreads, gardens and carvings over lintels and fireplaces. Some brought flowers or shells to Zeruah, hoping she could use them in her embroidering. The oldest man in town suggested that she look at the snowflakes. And he was pleased when he saw her putting one of these in her work. Even two lonely Indian students, who had been sent to study at the medical school in that town, drew designs for Zeruah's carpet — and added their initials. Somehow Zeurah managed to make people feel that the carpet she was fashioning belonged to them as well as to its maker.

Many marveled at the beauty of the girl Zeruah when she planned their tasks with them. Everyone forgot that once the girl had been thought plain. And, as for friendliness, where, the people of Castle Town would demand, could you find so friendly a person, and one with so great patience? And above all so cheerful. Why, she fairly radiated happiness!

As for the blue cat, during that year he spent most of his time in the different houses of Castle Town. And he sang and sang to everyone who would listen.

So that undoubtedly the blue cat's song had much to do with what happened. Though many spoke of the pulpit of Thomas Dake and of the influence they felt in the church — "peace as of pine trees and beauty as of cherry blossoms."

That year, too, nearly everyone drank tea from Ebenezer Southmayd's beautiful teapot or ate from the picture cloths of John Gilroy.

Less and less did folk speak of gold and power. And more and more they talked of beauty and peace and content. So that the spell of Arunah was pushed back and back until it disappeared beyond Bird Mountain, or was lost in the waters of Lake Bombazine. Instead, a brightness shone all through the valley, a brightness which was both glory and blessing from one end of Castle Town to the other.

When the blue cat was certain that the enchantment was as strong as he and the river's song could make it, he came back the main road, up the winding lane to Zeruah. The door was open and Zeruah herself was standing there to greet him.

"I knew you would come, blue cat," she said. "See, I have fashioned a hearth rug just for you. There you may lie as long as you live and sing your own song."

The blue cat entered, waving his tail. And as he looked up at Zeruah to purr his thanks he was astonished to see how beautiful she was. No wonder all Castle Town loved her.

So the blue cat — without a single black hair on him — curled himself down on the hearth rug and gazed about. It was a beautiful room to return to. He saw himself pictured on the carpet spread now on the floor. Not a beautiful cat perhaps, but one with character, he hoped. He saw the kittens of the barn cat there — really quite nice kittens at that. They would — the three of them — be on that carpet forever.

He thought of the quest he had finished, the task com-
pleted. And he stretched himself gratefully from tail to
paws to eartips. He had sung the song of the river and the
spell of that song lay over the valley.

The Bright Enchantment

*Today Castle Town in Vermont is a town of yesterday, a
town not built to seem like yesterday, a town not restored,
but kept. Castle Town is real.*

— Statement made by a recent visitor.

CHAPTER NINE

THE BRIGHT ENCHANTMENT

CASTLE TOWN *is* enchanted. Even as it was when the settlers came, bringing beauty and peace and content through the wilderness, so it is today.

The pride of Castle Town is in the pulpit in its church, which is the most beautiful pulpit in Vermont, and in the houses, porticoes, archways, and stairways which Thomas Royal Dake, the carpenter — the artist of yesterday — fashioned. Upon the whole town this man has set his touchmark as surely as Ebenezer Southmayd ever set his upon pewter.

The stranger, passing through, drives more and more slowly, until he stops and says: "There is a spell upon this place!"

Once a year the doors of the homes of Castle Town are opened, and all the beautiful treasures, which the song of the blue cat caused to be fashioned, are shown to strangers who come from far and wide to see them, and to hear the story of Castle Town.

Two things the visitors do not see. One is the teapot of Ebenezer Southmayd. Folk still speak of it, but no one knows what has happened to it, or where it may be hidden. The second treasure that is missing is the carpet which

Zeruah Guernsey fashioned. For that carpet, together with the hearth rug of the blue cat, hangs in the Metropolitan Museum of the City of New York.

If you doubt this story, you can go and see for yourself. In the daytime the blue cat will give you stare for stare. But at night, when the Museum is quite empty and a blue moon shines through the windows, then the blue cat's song may be heard echoing down every corridor.

Did not the river say he should live forever?

Arunah?

Scarce a soul remembers him. For his spell over Castle Town was completely vanquished, even as the river had hoped. Though, as the river had likewise promised, Arunah died to the tune of his own song of speed — crushed beneath the wheels of a train. Even today the sound of the train whistle through the valley is a sound to chill one's bones. It is all that remains of the dark enchantment.

As for the river which flows through the valley, go and sit beside it. And if you should hear it suddenly begin to sing its song, turn quickly. There in the reeds for an instant — if you are quick enough — you will see a small blue shadow. For of course it is hardly to be expected that the blue cat — who was no ordinary cat — stays in the Metropolitan all the time!

Sing your own song. Sing well! Sing well!

HOW THE BLUE CAT OF CASTLE TOWN
CAME TO BE WRITTEN

THE people of Castleto'n sing their own song to this day.

Not long ago reports reached Washington that on Grandpa's Knob, a high point above this Vermont town, what looked like a giant windmill turned great arms in the sun. It was said that this was a wind turbine, which was seeking to use the wind to generate electricity. So, in the summer of 1946, Catherine Coblentz went to Castleto'n with her husband, who was interested in seeing this experiment.

There at a church supper, Hulda Cole, the village librarian, told her that Castleto'n was noted as the site from which Ethan Allen set out to take Fort Ticonderoga, and that the town was justly proud of two of its early citizens. One was the carpenter who built there the most beautiful church pulpit in Vermont, as well as many of the town's beautiful houses. The second was a girl who had designed and fashioned a carpet so beautiful and unusual that it hung now in the Metropolitan Museum of New York. On that carpet, among other designs, was pictured a most fascinating blue cat.

"Why a blue cat?" inquired Mrs. Coblentz. But no one in all the town could say. Although there were those who recalled having heard that, in the days when the carpet lay on the floor of its creator's parlor, any cat walking into the room for the first time would always stop short, arch his back and spit at the blue cat pictured beneath his nose.

In the winter of 1946 Hulda Cole sent the source material of the town — which had been gathered by Mary Gerrish Higley and left to Mrs. Cole personally — to Catherine Coblentz in Washington. Its unexpected arrival was so tempting that Mrs. Coblentz studied it carefully, and twice returned to Castleto'n to see and learn more.

Not only was the history fascinating in itself — but the stuff of folklore was there. And so the author has handled it in this book. For a year and a half, she insists, the Blue Cat sat on her pillow night after night, trying to purr his story into her not-unwilling ears. Being a Vermonter by birth, Mrs. Coblentz was prepared to evaluate highly the spell which even to this day lies over this Vermont valley town. Every person mentioned in the book actually lived in the town, and did the things of which this book tells, and the names are the real names of those individuals of yesterday.

Or, to sum it up. Every word in the book is true, and there isn't a word of truth in it.

Acknowledgments :
To these people of Castleto'n:
> Mr. and Mrs. James Burns, Miss Edna Higley, Mrs. Raymond Ransom, Mrs. Custis St. John, Mrs. G. H. Taggart, who were generous with their homes and their knowledge; Mrs. Beatrice St. John Wright, for permission to sketch designs from one of the Gilroy tablecloths, now in her possession.
> To Mrs. Harold Brown, and Mrs. Margaret Onion for clarification of some final details; and to Mr. George

Hutchins and Mr. Jim Eaton, for help in ascertaining the location of the Mansion House.

To William Rice for making a map of early Castleto'n.

To Lawrence Ward for special assistance.

For reading the manuscript and making helpful suggestions:

Miss Karin Blanchard of New York City; and Herbert Wheaton Congdon of Arlington, an authority on Vermont architecture, and author of *Old Vermont Houses.*

For pictures and a reproduction of the touchmark of Ebenezer Southmayd:

Ledlie Laughlin, author of *Pewter in America, Its Makers and Their Marks.*

The interpretations of the characters in this book are derived from the source material, and are, of course, the author's — and the blue cat's!